# TROUBLE AT CLENCHERS MILL

By Diana J Febry

COVER DESIGN BY DIANA J FEBRY

Proofreading provided by the Hyper-Speller at https://www.wordrefiner.com

# CHAPTER ONE

Assuming it was the hospital and imagining the worst, Alicia Fielding shot upright when the telephone next to her bed rang. In her haste to grab the receiver, she knocked the phone from the bedside cabinet. She scrabbled to keep hold of the receiver and put it to her ear.

"Is Richard, there?"

Alicia seethed with anger. Typical, Cynthia! No introductions. Just barking demands. Glancing over at the clock, she saw it was only six o'clock. "Checking to see if your plan worked, are you?"

"Excuse me!"

"Sending him that dangerous horse. The vet is coming this morning to put it down," Alicia said.

"They will do no such thing! Put Richard on."

"He's not here. He's in hospital. No thanks to you and that crazy horse. You've gone too far this time, and I'll make sure you regret it."

"What are you talking about? Why is he in hospital?"

"Your evil horse tried to kill him."

"You're being ridiculous and overreacting as usual," Cynthia said. "The horse I sent was a perfect schoolmaster. I expect it simply spooked or lost its footing."

"No! It's dangerous!" Alicia shouted. "It nearly kicked me in the head when I was trying to return it to the stable after the accident. Only it wasn't an accident. You set it up."

"You're the crazy one." After a brief silence, Cynthia said, "Or maybe, clever. What did you do to the horse? Or did you swap it with a different one to get your grubby hands on his money?"

"I've had enough of this! Don't ever call here again. You'll be hearing from our Solicitor."

"Don't you dare hang up on me or speak to me in that manner! You do not put that horse down. It's evidence. I'll have my vet there as soon as I can arrange it to take blood samples. Then we'll see who tried to kill my ex-husband. Good day!"

Alicia stared at the dead receiver, livid with anger. She threw it across the room and climbed out of bed. There was no way she was going to get back to sleep, now. She pulled her mobile phone from the bedside cabinet drawer and rang Richard. The line was busy. Bloody Cynthia had beaten her to it.

# CHAPTER TWO

Kate Chapman slowed to a walk as she approached the Brook End crossroads. She bent double with her hands on her hips, willing the stitch to leave her side. The dull pain persisted, making each breath difficult. She walked in a small circle and looked back down Hangman's Hill. The last stretch had been dead straight. Or as straight as a British country lane can be. Lower down, the lane had been less steep as it snaked around the hill, giving the occasional glimpse of fields stretching into the distance as far as the eye could see. From where Kate now stood, sweating and panting, overgrown hedges and trees blocked the view to either side.

She grasped the cold metal of a nearby gate and pressed her hot forehead on the top rail. Running until she couldn't run anymore was her alternative to drinking in the same manner. She'd learnt the hard way there were two types of drinking. Sipping wine under a moonlit sky wrapped in her husband's arms, while planning the future. And gulping supermarket vodka, alone in her old bedroom in her parent's home. She'd gone from one state of inebriation to the other in a matter of weeks. In the wrong direction.

She started to walk the last mile to Holly Bush Farm, the relentless 'if only' thoughts intruding on her every step. Ignoring the pain in her side, she started to run. If only she could run fast enough to leave the voice behind. If only she hadn't told him to hurry home, her husband of two years wouldn't be dead. She'd be working for Manners Law Firm in accounts and living in Owl Cottage. Saving money so they could start a family. 'If only.'

The high stone wall surrounding Holly Bush Farm came into

sight. Strands of damp, brown hair that had escaped from her ponytail stuck to her face. She pushed herself harder and faster as she sped up along the length of the wall. She turned up the long driveway, past the empty paddocks. She slowed when she saw Simon Morris, sitting on an empty oil drum outside the vacant stables with his two black Labradors, Albert and Alfred, sprawled on the grass by his feet. If it hadn't been for a weird quirk of fate, Kate doubted they would have ever met. Simon was tall, muscular, handsome and rich, while she was plain and poor.

Looking annoyingly relaxed in designer jeans and a pale, blue T-shirt, Simon waved. "Hi. Enjoy your run?"

Kate came to a halt in front of him. Breathless, she gasped for air. She leaned forward, her hands finding her knees, as the two dogs excitedly licked her face. Pushing them away, she fondled their ears.

"You, see, I'm right," Simon said. "Exercise is not good for you. Hyped up lies in the media to make people feel inadequate and buy expensive Lycra clothing. What else could they use the material for? Running is especially bad for your knees. Did you know that? I've known people to have heart attacks in their twenties and thirties because of all that fitness nonsense." Sliding off the oil can, he asked, "Fancy a fry-up?"

Kate straightened and walked to the wrought-metal bench. "I'll sit a while until I get my breath back." Turning her face to the sun, she asked, "What have you been up to this morning?"

Simon followed her and sat cross-legged on the patch of grass in front of the bench. "Thinking, mostly. The world would be a better place if we all found time to simply think." Smiling, he added, "We had a great time in Europe, didn't we?"

Without looking at Simon, Kate replied, "We did, but we're back in England, now. I put a card in the post office in Brook End this morning. I'm a bit rusty, but hopefully, someone will want a groom. Just in case, I added that I'll do house-sitting, dog walking, gardening and general maintenance. Someone, somewhere must be desperate enough to need my services."

"You'll be inundated. I hope you made it clear you require

decent money. People around here are as tight as a duck's ass. They'll pay you way beneath the minimum wage if they can."

Kate shrugged. "I'll take what I can get. I bumped into a little, old lady in the post office called Glennis Potts. She seemed very pleasant and asked how you were."

Simon groaned. He snatched at a clump of grass and muttered, "Wonderful. She is not a sweet, old thing. She's a battle axe and the biggest gossip going. Tell me she's not going to visit us?"

"Umm. She did say she would pop around with a stew and some homemade cake."

"Great." Simon stood up. "We're going out for the day. She can leave it on the doorstep. Although it wouldn't surprise me if she has a key to the house."

"I'll need a shower first."

Simon shoved his hands in his pockets. "No big rush. She'll have to bake her damn cake first. I'm going to check out the barns, and then I'll start that fry-up." He turned back to Kate, "Hey! Did you put a card in the Post Office for me? Advertising my services as a private investigator?"

Kate shielded her eyes from the sun to look at him. "I thought we discussed this. I'm pretty sure you can't just say you're a private investigator and be one. Surely, you need qualifications and to register somewhere? And what about insurance?"

"Minor details." Simon waved away her practical concerns as he'd done before. "I can get all of that."

Kate watched Simon lope away. Before she knew better, she had assumed his lazy gait was a part of his free-spirited, carefree, beach-bum persona he'd been play-acting. Twenty-four hours ago, she'd learnt his laid-back manner was the swagger of a privileged background. He'd never had to worry about such mundane things as finding a job or running out of money. Sighing, she stood up from the bench and meandered her way to the back door. She made her way up the steep steps that led to the granny flat as Simon referred to it. At least he hadn't called it the staff area, which was probably closer to the truth.

Whatever his background, Simon had been a good friend and

an ever-present shoulder to cry on. He understood grief, having been through it himself with losing his parents. He rarely mentioned it, but he'd hinted that they'd also been involved in a car accident. She should be kinder to him. The problem was, since returning to England, everything fuelled her frustration and pent-up anger at the world for destroying her carefully planned life.

Kate dragged a crumpled pair of jeans and a T-shirt from her haversack. She sat heavily on the bed and flicked on her phone. She really should telephone someone to tell them she was home. Simply posting her return on Facebook wouldn't go down well. She hadn't looked at the site for months and doubted anyone bothered to check her profile, anymore. She couldn't bring herself to change the profile picture, but at the same time, she couldn't bear to see it. It showed her and Andrew making stupid faces for the camera. She snatched up her change of clothes, stomped to the bathroom and slammed the door on the outside world.

She stepped into the hot shower as she recalled how she'd met Simon after her disastrous trip to Irwin Mitch Solicitors, specialists in personal injury claims. In the dull office, painted magnolia with nondescript prints on the walls, the skinny, spotty twit in a suit named Hugh, droned on. 'Liability won't be an issue. The problem is your age. They'll try to limit the loss of earnings claim by saying you'll remarry. It's a shame you're childless. If there were children, we could claim up to their eighteenth birthday.'

Smart, sensible, quiet Kate had listened politely up until that point when a red mist had descended. She'd stood up and shouted, "You asshole!" and stormed from the room, slamming the door shut behind her as hard as she could.

She'd careered through corridors, her eyes blinded with tears of rage, with no idea where she was heading. Realising she had no idea which way was out, she had stopped in front of a notice board. With fists clenched, she had tried to control her emotions sufficiently to think straight for long enough to work out how to leave the building. She wasn't even sure which floor she was on. Breathing heavily, she had stared straight ahead, her vision blurred by tears. Gradually, the handwritten notice, in front of her face had started to make sense.

**Hey Guys. Been a blast. I'm off travelling tomorrow. Last chance for the adventure of your lifetime. There's space in the van if you or any of your friends fancy it. Simon.**

Underneath was a mobile phone number. Kate had ripped the note from the board and called Simon, a guy she had never met, and informed him if he could give his word, he wasn't a serial killer or a pervert, he had a co-adventurer.

After breakfast, Simon suggested they walk the dogs over to the Horseshoe Inn in a neighbouring village. "Now you've announced my return to Glennis, the whole area will know about it, so we may as well hit the hub of the local community. Neville always does a good pint."

"Sure," Kate replied, collecting the dirty plates and carrying them over to the sink.

"Leave them on the side," Simon said, collecting his boots from the back door.

Kate continued to swill the plates under the tap before placing them in the dishwasher. "Sorry, it's a bad habit I know, but I can't leave them out for someone else to find," she muttered.

Simon returned to his chair. Bending forward to lace his boots, he asked, "Umm, who do you think is going to find them?"

Closing the dishwasher door, Kate replied, "They're done, now. I'll get my boots." Returning to the table, she checked her phone. "No inundation of job offers yet."

"Give it a chance. You only put the ad up on the board a couple of hours ago. There's no rush." After watching Kate lace her boots, Simon said, "I thought you would go back to working in accounts."

"Financially, I'll have to eventually. For now, if I don't get a live-in groom's job, I can probably rent a small place nearby."

"You can stay here, as long as you like. I've already told you that. Stay forever, come to that. Makes no odds to me."

"Thank you, I appreciate the offer. Don't think I don't, but I want a place of my own. My own space. Somewhere that's mine."

"Renting isn't owning," Simon muttered under his breath.

"What was that?"

"Nothing. Are we good to go?" Simon replied, with a mock face of perfect innocence.

Typical of a British summer, clouds had quickly rolled in as the day progressed. The sun made only fleeting appearances as Simon led the way across the fields behind the house. He walked alongside Kate, missing the easy banter they had shared across Europe. Their ability to laugh while bumping into one another in the cramped camper van was very definitely a distant memory. The increased space of Holly Bush had put an even greater distance between them. He'd never been friends with a girl he'd not slept with before. To be fair, he'd never managed to stay friends with the girls he had slept with. Most of his relationships had ended up in a slap. His face doing the receiving, their palm doing the giving. Kate had provided a lot of firsts.

"I've been thinking. A dangerous pastime of mine, I know. I don't have the qualifications, experience or tools to be a private investigator, yet. But I need to start somewhere," Simon said. "I'll make another card tomorrow making that clear and put it next … no, underneath your card in the Post Office."

"There's no need to make fun of me," Kate replied. In a flat, resigned voice, she added, "You don't need a job. You never have."

Simon sighed. "But I'd like one."

"Then go ahead." A look of guilt spread across Kate's face. "Look, I'm sorry. Do what you want to do. What do I know, anyway?"

"You know lots of stuff," Simon replied, encouragingly. "Like accounts and how to speak French. How to pack everything you could ever need in an emergency into your bag. That's an amazing skill." He nudged Kate playfully. "Are you sure you didn't borrow your bag from Mary Poppins?"

Kate nudged him back. "Idiot."

"And you know about horses. I didn't know that."

Kate's smile disappeared. "I was pony mad as a child. I owned a horse briefly. Bought it cheaply from a woman too scared to ride him. I took him from not being able to walk in a straight line to competing at two-star events."

"What happened?"

"Nothing happened," Kate replied, clambering over a stile and marching off. "I sold him for the deposit on our home. Then we were saving up to start a family, but I rode out every weekend for a local point-to-point trainer. That was my horse fix for the week."

Simon jogged to keep up. "I hope you highlighted your ability to produce quality competition horses and deal with fit thoroughbreds on your card. You need to learn to big yourself up. Sell your unique skills."

"That's what you learn to do at posh school, is it?"

Stung by the comment, Simon fell quiet.

After a few strides, Kate said, "It sounds like you know a bit about horses? You're using the correct terminology."

Simon decided this wasn't the time to say he had excelled at playing polo, and replied, "I've got a rough grasp of the basics. But don't you want more of a challenge?"

Kate gave a small smile and a shrug. "I want a simple, straightforward groom's position for a short time before I return to the real world. No pressure. Think of it as another thing ticked off my bucket list."

"I get that. The no-pressure bit."

Kate marched on to the next stile. Instead of climbing over, Kate turned to sit on the top rail. "I'm sorry, I'm being a bit of a grump." Sighing, she added, "I guess I'm annoyed you lied to me about who you were."

Simon pulled a face. "I lied? When? And what about you? You told me you were a friend of Hugh Saunders."

"No, I didn't," Kate replied, indignantly. "I said I'd been to see Hugh, which I had. I never referred to him as a friend. You assumed that." A rustling in the hedge distracted her. A pheasant finally appeared and ran halfway across the field before remembering it could fly.

Simon laughed. "They're not the brightest. But come on. When did I lie to you?"

"Am I going in the right direction?" Kate asked, jumping down on the other side of the stile.

Simon climbed over after her and pointed to a clump of trees. "There's an old stone bridge across the river, just through there. Then one more field and we'll pick up the lane that drops down past a war memorial and into the village. About another twenty minutes and we'll be sitting in the beer garden. So? My dreadful lie?"

Walking on, Kate said, "You said your trip was being paid for by rental income on your home."

"Correct."

"You failed to mention your home was a mansion set in its own grounds."

"Hardly a mansion! It's an eight-bedroom farmhouse with a granny flat. Other than the few paddocks next to the house, the land is rented out to local farmers."

"Are we still on your land, here?"

"Yes. But, so what? I don't get how I lied to you about who I am. I'm the same person as before." Simon waved his arm dismissively. "All this. It was my parent's life. It doesn't change who I am."

Kate looked away. "I know. It was my interpretation that was wrong. It came as a shock, is all. The fact remains, I have to return to the mundane business of making enough money to feed myself and pay rent at some point."

"I've said, you can stay as long as you like."

"Until you find a suitable wife. Someone like you. You won't want me around then. Even if you think you will, your wife won't. I don't belong here."

"Neither do I, and I think you're getting a little ahead of yourself. Wife, family? Where are they coming from?"

"I know you think I'm being stupid. Maybe I am."

# CHAPTER THREE

They fell silent as they made their way down the steep incline to the Horseshoe Inn. The whitewashed building covered with overflowing hanging baskets reminded Kate of pubs she'd visited during trips to Devon and Cornwall with Andrew. She pushed the "if only" mantra away, swallowed the lump in her throat, forced a smile and marched on.

The clouds that had threatened rain earlier had disappeared, and the white of the building reflected the bright sunshine. She felt there should be the taste of salt in the air rather than the close, dry heat that pricked beneath her jacket. Or maybe she was thinking of the salty tears she'd fought back a few moments earlier. She took a deep breath and concentrated her mind on the here and now.

Her shame about her accusations created more prickly heat. Simon was right. He hadn't changed. She was being a bitch to him when all he'd ever shown her was kindness. Her black mood had come down hours before they arrived at Holly Bush Farm. The dread had started to build the moment they'd turned towards England. Once Simon announced his tenants had moved out without notice, and they were returning to England, she'd tried to fit her delayed acceptance that her husband was gone into one ferry crossing. It was hardly Simon's fault she was too weak and frightened to return to her family home.

When they entered the pub, chairs scraped across the stone floor, and a kaleidoscope of faces, young, old, male and female surrounded them. Kate was pushed to the sidelines as strangers crowded around Simon, welcoming him home like a long-lost son.

Feeling awkward, she painted on a smile as she stepped back to make room for Simon's friends. Comparing the situation to her likely muted welcome home was only going to depress her. Giving up on trying to catch Simon's eye, she turned towards the bar to catch the attention of the barman. A short, slight man with a shock of curly, black hair spotted her and propelled himself along the bar towards her on a wheeled stool. Shouting over the noise, she ordered two pints of lager and asked to see a bar menu. She didn't feel hungry, but she could pretend to study it as she stood alone at the far corner of the bar.

Taking her first sip from her pint glass, she was jostled from behind. The shove caused her to bash her teeth on the rim of the glass. Turning to see who had barrelled into her, her eyes widened. A plump, older woman with flowers stuck into an untidy bun wearing a huge medallion hung around her neck, smiled at her.

"You look terribly lost and alone, flower. Come and sit with us, darling," the woman boomed, waving her hand towards a small table set in a bay window. A giant of a man wearing white robes and open-toed sandals beamed encouragement.

"Umm. I'm not sure," Kate stuttered, wondering what bizarre cult they belonged to. "My friend will be over soon."

"That naughty, Simon! I'll have a word with him. Abandoning you in this dreadful way," the woman replied, still smiling from ear to ear.

Kate looked desperately around for Simon to save her. The woman's eyes were glazed, and alcohol fumes seeped from every part of her. Before she could think of an excuse, the woman lifted Simon's pint from the bar and, with her other hand steered Kate unwillingly to the table. "It's quite okay, petal. We don't bite."

The giant at the table bared his teeth before disintegrating into a high-pitched giggling fit. The woman swiped at him. "Behave yourself, Dick. Ladies are present."

Kate felt herself being pushed down onto a rickety, hard-backed chair. She twisted in the seat so she could see back across the bar. Simon remained engulfed by the crowd. All she could see was the top of his head. Realising he was not coming to her rescue any time soon she took a deep drink from her pint.

Dick patted her on the back, nearly sending her sprawling across the table, squirting out her mouthful of beer. "That's what I like to see. A woman with a hearty appetite."

Kate put down the glass for safety and glared at the man. She wasn't used to such rough handling from strangers, especially, ones who were so odd.

Oblivious to her annoyance, the woman said, "Oh, how awfully amiss of me. We haven't been properly introduced. I'm Gladys Deeeath, and this is the love of my life and, if I may add, my saviour Dick. But enough about me. What is your name, my lovely? And how do you know young Simon? I do hope you have been able to make him see past his awful tragedy. Heartbreaking for one so young to be touched by such dreadful sadness. Don't you think, Dick? Quite intolerable."

Wondering if she meant the death of Simon's parents or something more, Kate was about to ask when Simon appeared at the table.

"Hello, Gladys. Dick. Lovely to see you both." Collecting the two pints from the table, he added, "Sorry, I need to steal Kate away. I've some friends desperate to meet her. Catch you later."

Not needing any encouragement, Kate was on her feet and edging away when she bumped into a couple who were leaving. Turning around to apologise, she recognised one as an old school friend. "Fiona! What are you doing here?"

Looking equally surprised, Fiona replied, "I could ask you the same thing. The last anyone heard from you was that cryptic Facebook post you made about travelling the World."

Blushing, Kate replied, "Yes, I'm sorry about that. I've only just returned to England. Last night, in fact. Do you live here?"

The good-looking, older man tugged Fiona's arm. "We need to get going."

"Sorry, I've got to go. I'll message you later," Fiona said. "Reply this time."

Before Kate could say anything, Fiona was gone, and Simon

was steering her across the busy pub. He whispered in her ear, "Nobody is waiting. I thought you probably needed rescuing from our local Druid Masters."

"Oh! That's what they were," Kate replied, as she dodged around a group of men playing spoof.

"Harmless enough, but you don't want to take any notice of the nonsense they talk. I assume they pronounced their name as Deeeath?" When Kate nodded, he added, "Their name is Death, but they always insist that's not how it's pronounced."

They'd almost reached the rear door that led to the beer garden when a woman, dressed smartly in tailored tweed trousers and a short-sleeved blouse, intercepted them. "Excuse me. Are you the young lady who posted a card in the post office this morning? About seeking work with horses?"

"Yes. That was me," Kate replied. "How can I help you?"

Simon said over Kate's shoulder, "Hello, Mrs. Fielding. I'm going to be putting a card in too. Advertising my services as a private investigator."

Cynthia Fielding looked him up and down suspiciously. She gave a nervous laugh and said, "Perfect! Is there somewhere quieter we could talk? We appear to be blocking the entrance."

# CHAPTER FOUR

Once they were settled on a picnic bench in the beer garden, Cynthia looked nervously around but remained silent.

"Well? How do you think Kate can help you?" Simon asked.

Cynthia took a deep breath and said, "I'm probably being silly, but it just seems so strange. The horse that left here was an absolute gentleman. Nothing like the crazy beast *she* says arrived." She sighed heavily. "I didn't mean to cause such friction."

"Okay," Kate said slowly. "You've sold a horse, and the buyer isn't happy?"

"No. Nothing like that," Cynthia said, furiously shaking her head. "If that were the case, I would have it back tomorrow. I've asked for it to be returned, but it seems to have become more of an issue."

"Issue? Why don't you start at the beginning?" Simon suggested.

"As you know, I divorced Richard a few years back," Cynthia said, in a way that suggested she now regretted the decision. "He's since remarried and is settled in some fabulous place in Dorset. He rang me, asking if I could find him a suitable horse. The one I found came highly recommended by a good friend of mine. I kept it here a few days and rode it out to be sure it was safe. Happy it was, I sent it down to Richard. It is now a dangerous lunatic, according to his new partner, and Richard is in hospital with broken ribs. *She's* accused me of trying to kill him for the money. I'm convinced it's the other way around. I've booked a local vet to take blood samples from the horse, but I'd like someone on my side down there. I would go myself, but Alicia has staked her claim and made it abundantly clear that I'm not welcome." With a look of disgust and making the word sound something unsavoury, she added, "That's her name. Alicia."

"Blood tests! Are you suggesting the horse was drugged in an attempt to kill your husband?" Simon asked.

"That's exactly what I'm suggesting. Poor Richard! He has no idea what he's married to. Well, he's going to find out, now. I know the horse I sent was a well-mannered schoolmaster. I've always had a good relationship with Richard, and we amicably came to a good financial arrangement. We may have even got back together if it hadn't been for *her*. Alicia is using the situation against me. Claiming I wanted to kill Richard and other such nonsense."

"I'm guessing we're not going to be made very welcome there," Kate said.

"*She* tried to make things difficult, but I've settled everything with Richard. He suggested I send someone down in my place. It's his home, so you needn't worry about *her*."

"When did this accident happen?" Kate asked.

"Yesterday. I've been on to the vet all morning, arranging the tests. First, they said they needed Madame Alicia's agreement, and then they insisted I pay for the tests up front as I'm not registered with them. Finally, they agreed to take the tests if I was happy to pay their ludicrously inflated call-out charge because it's the weekend. I came in here to settle my nerves. I believe it's fate I saw your note in the post office on my way here and then bumped into you."

Kate forced herself not to flinch when Cynthia laid her cold hand, swollen and deformed by arthritis, over hers. Looking up into her heavily lined face, she did her best not to inhale the fumes from her breath. Alcohol was more likely to seep from her pores than tears leak from her cold, steely eyes.

"I'm surprised he ended up with her," Cynthia continued. "He always desperately wanted a son. The fact I only produced baby girls left me feeling inadequate. She only has a daughter. Maybe *she's* not too old to try again. There was a young man once," Cynthia said, her voice trailing away.

Kate wasn't sure whether Cynthia was suggesting she'd had an affair or if Richard had a son with another woman. Cynthia was back in full flow, giving her no chance to interrupt and ask. Kate's hand was being pounded by Cynthia's, so she slipped it from the table and put it in her lap out of harm's way.

"It was after the young man's funeral that he changed," Cynthia continued. "He said there was more to life and acted as though I had clipped his wings in some way. That's when he ran off with *her.* Can you help me?"

Before Kate could say anything, Simon said, "Of course we can. We'll leave once you've signed our agreement and settled the introductory fee. We'll come over to yours later with the paperwork. Will that give you time to contact Richard and say we're on our way?"

"Yes, yes. That will be splendid." Cynthia raised her wine glass to chink with Simon's pint glass. "Cheers. Here's to a happy resolution of this piece of unpleasantness."

# CHAPTER FIVE

Stuffing her clothes into her holdall, Kate complained, "I can't believe you've talked me into this."

"Oh, ye of little faith. It'll be fun. You are going to help like you promised, aren't you?" Simon asked.

Zipping up her bag, Kate replied, "I said I would, and I will. Just this once, until I get work of my own lined up. But fun? You know we probably won't be allowed anywhere near the place. And I'm not entirely convinced the vet will be happy to tell us anything directly. Even if she is, and the blood tests show something was given to the horse, what then?"

"We investigate and discover who drugged the horse, of course, silly," Simon replied. "The new wife, Alicia, has to be the number one suspect."

"What if the blood tests come back negative?"

"We establish whether it is the same horse that Cynthia sent and whether anything else could have caused the out-of-character behaviour."

Lifting her bag off the bed, Kate said, "I still think this is a crazy idea, but I'm good to go. Once you've telephoned Alicia to confirm she is expecting us and won't chase us off their land with a shotgun."

Simon quickly checked his watch. "Cynthia should have contacted her by now." He pulled out his mobile and called the number he'd been given, while Kate sat on the edge of her bed to wait. He ended the call with a smug smile. "All sorted. She's looking forward to meeting us."

Looking doubtful, Kate said, "And the vet?"

After completing that call, Simon said, "Cynthia has already spoken to her. She'll pass on the results as soon as she hears back from the lab. She expects that it will be in a day or so." Holding his arm out towards the door, he added, "Shall we?"

Shaking her head, Kate picked up her bag. "Do you always get your own way?"

Simon grinned and threw her the keys to the camper van. "Load your bag up while I round up the dogs and make sure everything here is locked up."

◆ ◆ ◆

As they drew closer to Richard Fielding's new home, the lanes became narrow and twisty, plunging them up and down steep inclines with hairpin bends. Luckily, they met no other vehicles, as passing places were few and far in between. As they were warned, the satnav became erratic. Whether it was the lack of signal between the high banks lining the lanes or it was confused by the twists and turns was open to debate.

Kate pulled the handwritten directions Alicia had given Simon from the dashboard. "I think we're nearly there. We should pass a church and a pub called the Wind Whistle Inn, shortly, where we turn left down a steep hill. At the bottom, there is a crossroads. We turn right, and their property will be about a mile along that lane."

"Alicia said, we can't miss it. It's surrounded by a high stone wall, and the entrance gates should be open for us." Grinning across at Kate, Simon added, "A clear sign we are welcome. And let's face it, Mrs. Fielding, number two can't be any scarier than number one."

The directions proved accurate, and a few minutes later, they were turning onto the driveway for Clenchers Mill. The grass on either side of the drive would make the average golfer green with envy. Newly erected post-and-rail fencing separated it from the natural meadowland, full of wildflowers and butterflies.

The view in front of them could have been copied from a biscuit tin lid. Surrounded by a low stone wall, the front garden was a mass of colours where hollyhocks, foxgloves, lavender, buddleias and rose bushes clamoured for space. A rambling red rose covered the whitewashed walls of the house. The sound of a giant, wooden water wheel attached to the side of the house slowly turning, along with the heavy scent of flowers, was intoxicating.

Leaving the camper van unlocked on the drive, Simon opened the wrought metal gate to the front garden. "Shall we?"

Kate took a deep breath of the scented air and blew out her cheeks. Hesitating, she looked up at the house and said, "I don't think I've ever seen such a beautiful place. I feel like I'm intruding."

Simon held the gate open for her looking impatient.

Kate shook her head. "I'm not sure this is such a good idea."

Before Simon could respond, the front door opened, and Alicia Fielding stepped onto the porch. "Simon and Kate?"

One look at Alicia and Kate felt like running in the opposite direction. Cynthia had referred to Alicia as a gold-digging, trophy wife, scheming to have her and her daughters written out of her wealthy, ex-husband's will. The stunning house had reinforced this viewpoint, and Kate had imagined Alicia to be attractive but also pretentious and guarded. Certainly, hostile to their involvement.

The woman gracefully strolling to meet them wore ripped designer jeans and a faded, blue sweatshirt. Her feet were bare, and her dark hair was tied in a knot with loose strands framing her face. Her pretty, oval face was void of makeup, wearing only a wide smile. If Kate had spent three hours in front of a mirror trying to perfect the look, she would have looked scruffy. This woman had nailed effortless stunning beauty. Alicia had the type of casual beauty men drooled over while women had to fight the urge to scratch her eyes out. Even her slightly crooked front tooth added to her mesmerising charm and hint of hidden vulnerability.

Forced or natural, Alicia's smile made Kate instinctively smile back. With aching cheeks retaining the smile, Kate couldn't help thinking it was no wonder Richard would prefer the second Mrs Fielding to the forthright, domineering Cynthia. There was no comparison between the two women. Kate blushed when Alicia held out her arm in greeting.

"Hi, lovely to meet you both," Alicia purred.

She sounded genuine, yet Kate sensed their presence was unwanted. Alicia's brown eyes were as alluring as the rest of her, but they were guarded and suspicious. Underneath the elegance and poise, Kate sensed something darker lurking. She detected hostility and anxiety, maybe even panic. When Alicia added, "I hope you found the place without too much trouble?" Kate noticed Alicia constantly flicked her forefinger and thumb together, and she wasn't looking at them, but searching the grounds behind them. Kate fought the impulse to look over her shoulder to see who could be hiding in the bushes. The woman's lover, desperate to leave unseen, possibly.

"No problem, at all. Your directions were excellent," Simon replied.

Kate gave him a sideways glance. His expression confirmed he'd fallen hard for the woman's charms.

"Thank goodness, for that," Alicia replied, in her singsong voice. "Because I'm rather ashamed to say your trip was quite unnecessary."

Kate thought, 'Oh, here we go. The charm offensive was devised to knock us off course. Now, she'll demand we leave her property.'

Alicia bowed her head and said, "I was in shock after the accident, and I'm afraid I was very rude to Cynthia. I intend to call her later today to apologise."

"That is very good of you, but as we're here, we might as well wait to speak to the vet once she has the test results," Kate replied. "Cynthia has already paid for them."

"Yes, of course," Alicia replied, staring intently at Kate for the first time.

Kate withered under her scrutiny, deciding she preferred it when her attention was drawn elsewhere.

Breaking eye contact, Alicia said, "I'll show you where you can stay overnight. Follow me."

"We've brought my two dogs with us. We're happy to sleep in the camper van," Simon offered humbly.

Kate rolled her eyes, surprised he hadn't fallen at the woman's naked feet.

"It's up to you," Alicia said dismissively. "Your dogs are very welcome to stay in the cottage."

Kate walked behind, trying to work out Alicia. She appeared open and relaxed as she chatted freely with Simon about her plans for setting up self-catering holiday cottages on the property. Was she really going to apologise to Cynthia? She recalled Cynthia's suggestion that Alicia could have drugged the horse to make it behave in the way it did. Looking around her, it seemed obvious that if something were to happen to her new husband the economic windfall would be substantial. Alicia already had Simon eating out of the palm of her hand, hanging on her every word. Somebody had to stay level-headed and immune to her charms.

Finding Simon's adoration nauseating, Kate turned her attention to the grounds attached to the property. In the paddock to their right, a large, grey horse and two small ponies stood together under the shade of oak trees, their tails occasionally swishing away flies. Kate caught up with Alicia and Simon. "Is that the horse in question, Coolcaum Paddy?"

"Yes, I was about to point him out to you. The two ponies are from a local rescue centre. Would you like to check him over now?"

Kate glanced across at the horse. He looked like the one she'd seen in Cynthia's photograph album, but she wanted to take her time to compare him carefully. Her initial impression from a distance was that he looked peaceful and relaxed with the smaller ponies and had the solid, dependable stamp typical of an Irish Draught, Thoroughbred cross. More likely to be stubborn and lazy if he wanted to be uncooperative rather than turn himself inside out. "I'll pop back later to take a look rather than hold you up, if that's okay?"

"Of course. But please, be careful. I don't want any more accidents," Alicia replied, before continuing along the path. "Here we are," she announced, as they reached the end of a long, Cotswold-stone stable block converted into three terraced cottages. She produced a key and unlocked the front door to the end cottage. Handing the key to Simon, she said, "I'll leave you to settle in. If you need anything, please come over and ask. Would you care to come over for your evening meal later? At about seven o'clock?"

"That's a very kind offer," Simon replied, grinning from ear to ear, clearly smitten.

"We don't want to put you to any trouble," Kate said.

"It would be no trouble at all. You'd be doing me a favour. Richard isn't allowed home until after the doctor sees him tomorrow. My daughter, Helen, is staying with a friend for a little while. We thought her being elsewhere would be for the best. I could do with some company."

"If you're sure?" Kate replied, wondering how much of the offered hospitality had been forced on Alicia by Richard. She couldn't shake the suspicion that Alicia had been watching someone else leave the property earlier. Their untimely arrival may have deprived Alicia of her preferred company. Especially with her daughter conveniently staying with friends.

"We'd love to. We'll come over just before seven," Simon said firmly.

They waved to Alicia before entering the cottage to explore. Inside was oozing rustic charm. The old stone walls that had previously housed horses had been left un-plastered and colourful rugs covered the stone floor. The cosy living room contained a well-stuffed sofa and armchairs covered in matching tartan material, a sturdy coffee table and a side cabinet. A flat-screen television was mounted on the facing wall. On the remaining walls hung watercolours of the surrounding countryside. A small, white card tucked into the frame of each gave the details of the local artist and location.

In a small alcove, tucked almost out of sight, was a computer desk and chair. A laptop sat on the shelf. Pinned on a small cork noticeboard was the wi-fi password, brochures of local tourist attractions and menus from various local pubs and restaurants. Kate rifled through them, searching for the menu for the Wind Whistle Inn they'd passed in the village. Not finding one, she opened the folder placed next to the laptop. Inside were local Ordnance Survey maps with suggested walks marked with a highlighter pen.

The door adjacent to the nook led them into a small, well-designed, modern kitchen. On the side counter was an ice bucket containing a bottle of Moet. A thick, white card propped up next to it, read, 'Enjoy!'

"What a kind and thoughtful touch!" Simon said. "What do you think of Alicia? Hardly the wicked, husband-stealing witch that Cynthia described. I think she's lovely."

Kate mumbled, "You've changed your tune since we arrived. I thought she was your number one suspect. Looks can be deceptive, you know? Until we have a clearer idea of what caused Richard's accident, we should be wary of her."

Pretending he hadn't heard the comment, Simon said, "I'll drive the van around while you explore upstairs."

As Kate headed up the narrow, steep staircase, she said, "I might go for a run."

"Suit yourself. I'll probably do something far more sensible, like see if we've got Netflix and take a nap."

# CHAPTER SIX

At ten to seven, Kate and Simon made their way to the main house. The evening air was heavy with the scent of flowers, and the sound of water cascading over the waterwheel added to the tranquillity. Kate couldn't deny Alicia's taste was impeccable, and she could envisage people clamouring to stay in the holiday cottages and wanting to return year after year.

Although Alicia wasn't exactly what she was expecting and appeared friendly, she remained suspicious. She could have her pick of handsome men, and she was years younger than Richard. The attraction being his wealth, was a fair assumption. No one was as sweet and perfect as she appeared to be. Approaching the front door, the aroma of something delicious cooking suggested Alicia was also an accomplished cook.

When Simon rapped his knuckles on the front door, it swung open.

"Come on in," Alicia's voice called from inside. "No need to stand on ceremony." She joined them as Simon closed the door behind them.

Kate found herself walking in small circles, looking up in wonder. She'd never been invited into such a grand entrance hall. She stopped herself for fear she would damage the beautifully patterned stone-tiled floor. The walls were painted white, which contrasted with the rich tones of an impressive oak staircase leading to a galleried, second-floor landing. A stained glass, floor-to-ceiling window covered half of the wall, flooding the room with coloured, dancing light.

"This way," Alicia said. "It's such a beautiful evening. I thought we'd eat outside."

Kate gave an involuntary gasp as they entered an enormous living room. An archway to the side led to a dining area, dominated by a large table with seating for twelve. Beyond the table, running along the far wall, behind glass, was the internal mechanism of the water wheel. Unable to stop herself, Kate gushed, "Your house is amazing!"

"Thank you. I absolutely love it. It was tumbled down and filthy when we bought it. During the renovations, my priority was to protect and enhance the natural beauty of the remaining original features," Alicia said proudly.

"You've certainly achieved your aim," Kate replied. "I love the water wheel."

"We could eat in here if you prefer?" Alicia offered.

Through the open door at the end of the room, Kate could see a table set up on the patio. "Outside will be perfect. It would be a terrible shame not to take advantage of the warm weather we're having."

Alicia proved herself to be an entertaining and accomplished host as well as a fantastic cook, and Kate had to remind herself not to fall under the woman's spell throughout the delicious, vegetarian meal. Once they'd finished eating and were drinking coffee while enjoying the view over the landscaped rear garden, Kate said, "I met a friend of yours when I went for a run earlier."

Simon gave Kate a quizzical look, before shrugging. "Kate does like to punish herself with keep-fit nonsense."

Alicia's Royal Doulton cup clattered into its saucer. Her shaking hand caused brown liquid to spill from either side.

"Sue, from the village," Kate quickly said. "She asked me to pass on how sorry she was about Richard's accident. You're to call her if you need help with anything."

"Oh, her," Alicia said. Looking relieved, she re-lifted her teacup and took a sip.

"Were you expecting it to be somebody else?" Kate asked, trying to sound and look innocent.

Alicia lowered her cup and preoccupied herself with blotting the coffee dripping from its base. Simon gave Kate a sharp kick under the table and a stern look suggesting she should drop whatever she was getting at. He'd already poured scorn on Kate's theory the daughter had been sent away so Alicia could spend the evening alone with her mysterious boyfriend.

Kate decided not to press the matter any further, temporarily, at least. It was obvious that Alicia was rattled by the idea she'd spoken to someone from the village and had automatically assumed it was somebody else. She had every intention of following up on it later. "Maybe we could talk about Richard and the horse accident?"

"Yes, of course," Alicia said. "It was very kind of you to wait until now to ask. You've been such pleasant company and stopped me from constantly dwelling on the dreadful accident. Poor Richard. I can't wait to bring him home tomorrow, although the doctors say a full recovery will take some time."

"Did you telephone Cynthia earlier to apologise, like you said you would?" Kate asked.

"There was no answer. I will try again tomorrow. Please, rest assured that I do intend to make a full apology and withdraw those nasty accusations I made. Unfortunate timing all around. Cynthia can be very abrasive at the best of times. She rang to ask how the horse was settling at the wrong moment. I was worried sick about Richard, and it was a knee-jerk reaction. I was still in shock."

"So, you're not accusing Cynthia of anything?" Simon asked.

Alicia shook her head. "I'm sorry you've had a wasted journey."

"Your hospitality and that meal made it all worthwhile," Simon replied.

"Thank you. I had hoped you wouldn't be too cross with me," Alicia replied. Her childish tone set Kate's teeth on edge.

"All the same, I think we should wait to hear the results of the blood tests," Kate reminded Simon of their earlier agreement. Turning to Alicia, she continued, "I went out to the paddock to see Coolcaum Paddy. He seemed very placid and amiable. Is that how he normally is?"

Alicia sighed and said, "We've been calling him just Paddy," before raising herself from the table. She disappeared inside the house briefly, returning with a bottle of brandy and three glasses. She poured three good measures and re-took her seat. "Unless I had seen the way he behaved that day with Richard, I would have described him as a gentle giant. I was with Richard when he tacked him up that morning, and I waved to them as they plodded off along the driveway with no concerns whatsoever."

"What happened next?" Simon asked.

"I'd gone inside to collect my gardening gloves and was heading out to the garden when I heard a high-pitched whinny. It sounded more like a petrified scream from a horror movie. A clattering of hooves followed it. I looked up to see Paddy riderless with the stirrups waving about his sides, careering along the drive towards me. He was lathered in sweat, foaming at the mouth and rolling his eyes. He skidded on the corner and went down on his side. He floundered on the floor as if he was having a fit. He scrambled back up, sending gravel up like a spray of bullets and galloped towards the stable block. I ran after him and caught sight of him darting into his box. I managed to slam the door shut and slide the bolts across before he turned and barged the door with his chest.

"I've been around horses most of my life, but I've never seen a horse look so crazy, as he repeatedly threw himself at the door. He then started to rear, striking out over the door with his front legs. Timing it just right, I slammed and bolted the top door shut. I could still hear him crashing about and snorting inside, but at least he was contained. At that point, I was more concerned about finding Richard than the horse's welfare."

"It must have been terrifying," Simon empathised. "You did very well to get the doors bolted. You could have been trampled."

"In the heat of the moment, I didn't think about my safety. I have re-lived the moment when his front feet missed my head by millimetres on several occasions, since then. At the time, my priority was to find Richard. I left the horse and started to run along the drive. There were skid marks on the drive, and it looked like Paddy had fallen when he turned towards home. I carried on running and saw Richard on his side, in the recovery position, in the middle of the road. A car was parked nearby, and the driver was knelt by Richard. The emergency services appeared shortly after. I assumed the paramedics arranged for the helicopter. Everything seemed to be happening both at warp speed and in slow motion."

"Did you go with him in the helicopter?" Kate asked.

"No. The car driver kindly gave me a lift." Alicia got up and walked into the kitchen. She returned with a piece of paper and handed it to Simon. "Here is his telephone number. His first name is Mark. I didn't think to ask his surname in all the hullabaloo. I don't know how I can ever thank him enough. His quick thinking probably saved Richard's life."

Simon slipped the paper into his shirt pocket. "I'll call him tomorrow. Do you know if he saw what happened?"

Alicia shook her head. "He said he arrived afterwards."

"It might be that it was his driving that spooked the horse," Kate suggested. "Although, without witnesses, he's not likely to admit to it." Turning to Simon, she added, "He might not be keen to talk to us."

Alicia frowned. "That has crossed my mind, but I believed him when he said he had done nothing to upset Paddy. He was incredibly kind, and I would prefer you didn't accuse him of causing the accident without any proof. He was so helpful and friendly. And you didn't see how Paddy behaved. He didn't calm down until the following morning. If a car had spooked him, I would have expected him to have calmed down within half an hour."

"I was going to ask you about that. When did you check on the horse, again?" Kate asked.

"After I returned from the hospital. It would have been getting on for eight o'clock in the evening. Once I was satisfied that Richard was in safe hands and not going to die, I started to feel guilty about the way I had left Paddy locked in the stable. I called a taxi to take me home, intending to remove his tack and give him some hay and water. I heard him still thrashing around as soon as I walked into the yard. When I opened the top door, he was covered in sweat and relentlessly pacing around the stable. I managed to pull the bridle over his head from outside the stable. I didn't think it safe to go inside to remove the saddle. It was already ruined and covered in scuff marks. I threw some hay over the door and slipped a bucket of water in through the door. Then I returned to the house to call a vet out. To be honest, at that point, I was suggesting Paddy should be destroyed."

"What changed your mind?" Kate asked.

"The vet didn't arrive for another hour. When she did, Paddy was calming down. Calm enough for her to give him a sedative and remove the saddle. We decided as the horse appeared comfortable, we would put the decision off until the morning."

"And the following morning?"

"I was woken first thing by Cynthia's telephone call. I'd been awake most of the night and had only just dropped off to sleep. Cynthia demanded I do no such thing and insisted blood tests were taken. When I checked Paddy after her phone call, he appeared exhausted. He has been quiet and docile ever since."

"What does Richard say happened?" Simon asked.

"He doesn't remember anything after having breakfast that morning until he woke up in hospital. The doctors can't say whether he will remember anything more as he recovers."

"It does seem very strange the horse should have reacted so violently even if the car did spook it. Cynthia described Paddy as bombproof in traffic. Does anyone else have access to the horses? A groom, maybe?" Kate asked.

"No. I brought him in from the field about an hour before Richard was due to ride. He was quiet and relaxed, and there was nothing about his behaviour that gave me any concerns."

"Was there anyone else here? A gardener, maybe?" Simon suggested.

"No. Nobody. It's just us." Alicia stifled an involuntary yawn. Blushing, she apologised. "Sorry. It has been a long day."

"No need to apologise. Could I ask one more question before we go?" As Alicia nodded, Simon carried on, "Do you or Richard have any enemies? Someone who would like to harm you?"

Alicia looked as though Simon had slapped her in the face. She quickly dropped her gaze to the table. "No. Nobody like that. I shouldn't have kept you here so late. As I said, I'm not accusing Cynthia of anything. It was just a heat-of-the-moment thing about a freak accident. I'll be collecting Richard in the morning, but feel free to stay as long as you like tomorrow."

Simon and Kate stood to thank Alicia for her hospitality. Kate said, "Cynthia also asked us to find out if you wanted her to take the horse back?"

"Because of everything that happened, I would prefer him gone, but the final decision is Richard's," Alicia said.

Once they were out of earshot, Simon said, "Looks like I'm going to get some relevant private investigator experience after all. Good thinking about asking who else had access to the horse. From Alicia's description, it does sound like it was drugged in some way."

"We'll wait to see if the blood tests reveal anything, but if the horse was drugged, Alicia is the most likely candidate. It would be worthwhile finding out the details of Richard's will."

Simon hunched his shoulders and pushed his hands deeper into his trouser pockets. "I thought she was friendly and kind. Not the grasping gold digger Cynthia described, at all. She is genuinely upset about the accident. She admitted no one else came near the horse that morning. If she'd planned the accident, don't you think she would have done it when other people were around so she could spread the blame? She doesn't appear to have any idea why the horse behaved the way it did. She made the accusations when she was in shock, and she's going to apologise to Cynthia."

"She backed down *after* Cynthia arranged the blood tests and Richard told her to play nicely. Honestly, Simon! If you want to be an investigator, you'll have to start thinking with your brain," Kate said. "I find it very strange she decided to send her daughter away. Doesn't that strike you as odd and a bit suspicious?"

"Not really, no. You took an instant dislike to her on sight."

Kate shook her head and continued walking. "I'm tired, and I'm going up to bed."

Catching up to her, Simon said, "I don't think she's the type to do that sort of thing. She didn't even want us to upset the driver who possibly caused the accident."

Opening the front door, Kate replied, "For all we know, he's Alicia's lover and is in on it."

"Now you're being silly."

"I am simply suggesting possible scenarios. If the horse was drugged, and we won't know until tomorrow, Alicia is the only person who could have done it. This place is worth a fortune. I'm guessing Richard is of a similar age to Cynthia." Kate struck a thoughtful pose and rubbed her chin. "I wonder what the attraction is?"

"You're making assumptions because you're jealous of wealth. You know nothing of Alicia's background. She might be loaded, herself."

"And as little Lord Fauntroy, you'd know all about how to recognise the correct social class to mix with," Kate replied angrily, before stomping towards the stairs. "I'm tired, and I'm going to bed."

Simon leant his forehead on the bannisters. "Sorry. I didn't mean to offend you." Unsure whether Kate had heard him, he wandered into the kitchen and pulled a chilled bottle of Becks from the fridge. Sleep, when he was wound up, was impossible. He dropped onto one of the armchairs in the living room and flicked through the television channels. As the programmes clicked by, he went over the last few minutes in his head, trying to find the moment things turned personal and angry. No matter which way he looked at it, things could have been turned around right up to when he mentioned Kate's attitude to wealth. He pointed his first two fingers to his temple and pulled an imaginary trigger. Not the best way to win over her heart.

Kate rose early and decided to go for a run before facing Simon. She laced her trainers and opened the front door. The sky was a perfect blue, and the sun was shining, although there was a sharp chill in the air. She quietly closed the front door and performed a series of stretches before breaking into a gentle run.

She was in a relaxed rhythm by the time she'd rounded the corner and headed along the main driveway. Her trainers made a satisfying crunch on the gravel as she approached the closed five-bar gate.

She tugged at the gate's catch, but it didn't budge. Thinking it was stiff, as it looked brand new, she repositioned herself to the side and gave it a sharp pull. Still nothing. She peered closer, looking for a locking mechanism of some sort that was preventing it from opening. Seeing nothing, she sighed and started to climb over. She screamed when she was on the third rung and jumped back away from the gate in shock.

She quickly gathered her thoughts. Despite feeling sick, she looked closer at the gate. Not entirely comprehending what she was seeing, she turned to run back to the cottage to collect Simon. Alicia would be leaving in a few hours for the hospital. The last thing she needed was to discover her gate had been glued shut and two dead crows hung from the branches of the adjacent tree.

# CHAPTER SEVEN

Simon stumbled out his bedroom door, rubbing the sleep from his eyes. "What the hell? Is the house on fire?"

His face became animated as Kate described the scene at the gate. He disappeared and reappeared, pulling on his jeans and yesterday's T-shirt. Pulling out his penknife from a back pocket, he asked, "Have you got any nail polish remover with you?"

Frowning, Kate replied, "I think there's some in my makeup bag. Why?"

"It's the only thing I know that dissolves super glue."

"Really? How …?"

Simon replied, "Gluing people's lockers shut was a thing in my school." Holding out the penknife, he added, "Take this. Grab a sponge and the nail polish remover, and I'll meet you at the gate. I saw a ladder in the garden last night."

He was relieved his face hadn't betrayed the emotions that memories of the vile boarding school evoked. He was new money and hadn't been through the proper prep schools. His was the only locker routinely glued shut. No one was more surprised than him when his natural talent for polo and fencing was discovered, and most of the bullying stopped. Even then, a few boys carried on, pointing out that his family had probably fought for their ancestors, rather than alongside them.

Taking the knife, Kate said, "Are you planning to remove everything? Shouldn't we leave the scene as it is until the local police have seen it?"

"It's probably the work of local bored teenagers. The police aren't going to come rushing out with their sirens blaring, and Alicia needs to get through the gate to pick up Richard. She can report it later," Simon said, heading down the stairs.

Kate pocketed the knife and ran to her bedroom to grab the other things. Running back along the drive towards the gate, she caught up with Simon struggling to jog while carrying a metal step ladder. Kate grabbed one end of the ladder, and they ran together towards the gate. As they approached, Kate said, "I've brought my phone as well. I want to take some photographs. Alicia can show them to the police."

Simon set up the ladder, while Kate photographed the gate and the hanging crows from every angle. Once she slipped her phone into the pocket of her jogging trousers, she said, "What if this is somehow connected to Richard's accident?"

Simon started to climb the ladders and said, "Are you saying that you think Richard's accident was nothing to do with Alicia?"

Kate avoided replying by saying, "She needs to contact the police about this."

From halfway up the ladder, Simon said, "Hand me the knife. You get started with the nail polish remover."

Twenty minutes later, the birds were cut down and Kate had managed to pry off enough of the glue for them to force the gate catch open. Kate turned to look at the dead birds thrown onto the path. "What are we going to do with them?"

Simon picked the birds up with the end of the baler twine they were still attached to. "Unless you're going to make a bird pie, I'll chuck them in the bin."

"No! We need to keep them. As evidence."

"Okay, I'll find somewhere to put them." Lifting the birds, Simon asked, "Which would you prefer to carry back? These or the ladder?"

Kate folded the ladder and picked it up in response.

Walking back, they discussed who might have been responsible for the gate and whether it was connected to the horse's violent episode. Simon still thought it highly likely teenagers were responsible, but they agreed someone in the village might resent them moving in, and that would also explain Alicia's reaction to Kate talking to a local.

Approaching the house, Kate said, "We might as well tell Alicia about the gate, now."

"It can wait until she returns home with Richard. Together, they can tell us whether they've experienced similar things. If somebody has a major problem with them, they should have some inkling who it is."

Kate said. "If they do, I don't understand why they haven't reported anything to the police. Richard could have been killed. It possibly explains why Alicia has sent her daughter away to stay with a friend."

They walked around to the back of the cottage, where Simon found an empty recycling crate. He threw the dead birds in and slammed the lid shut. "Let's have a cooked breakfast. If the vet hasn't called by ten o'clock, we'll contact her. Once we know for sure whether the horse was drugged, we can have our talk with Alicia and Richard."

They were in the courtyard enjoying the morning sunshine when the vet rang. She indicated there was something amiss, but she wanted to discuss the results in person and take another set of samples. She ended the call saying she would be with them within the hour.

Kate got up from the table. "I'll go and let Alicia know. Technically, we can't give permission for more tests. Only the owner can."

"Poppycock! The vet has already been involved. These are just follow-up tests."

"I'm not so sure," Kate replied, with a worried look. "If Alicia is against more tests, we can't overrule her."

"The tests are at the request of Cynthia, don't forget. Cynthia is paying the vet and us to make sure everything is done properly."

"I guess. We still need to let Alicia know what is going on. She might want to delay collecting her husband until after the vet's visit."

They both turned towards the sound of a car engine starting up. The cottage blocked their view of the main house, but they both assumed it was Alicia leaving for the hospital. Kate shot up from her chair, saying, "I'll try to catch her before she leaves."

By the time she'd reached the front of the cottage, Alicia was approaching the main gates. Kate waved to her, knowing the distance was too far for her shouts to be heard, but Alicia didn't look back.

Kate returned to the cottage to find Simon rinsing their plates in the sink in the kitchen before loading them into the dishwasher. "I missed her," she said to the back of his head. "Can you give me her number so that I can call her?"

"Sure," Simon replied, bringing the number up on his phone before handing it over.

Kate tried the number twice without a reply.

Simon commented, "Someone's obeying the law about not answering their phone when driving."

"I'll try her later," Kate replied, handing back the phone. "Meanwhile, I'll go and get Paddy in for the vet. It'll be rather embarrassing if the vet turns up and we can't catch him."

"Hang on," Simon said, drying his hands on a tea towel. "I'll come with you. The vet didn't say why she wanted to take more tests. Maybe he has a tumour or something along those lines that makes him unpredictable."

# CHAPTER EIGHT

The vet arrived ten minutes early and drove directly to the small stable yard. With her tall figure and mane of black curls, she managed to look attractive in her green boiler suit and wellingtons. She greeted them with a broad smile and a firm handshake. "Hi, I'm Tammy. Is Alicia not around?"

Simon was too taken with the vet's attributes to respond. Kate gave him a sideward look and replied, "Unfortunately not. She's collecting her husband from the hospital. We understood you were happy to deal with us?"

"Yes, of course. You're here to represent the woman who sold the horse?"

Kate nodded. "We are. Our client is Cynthia Fielding, Richard's first wife. The horse was a gift from her, which is why the situation is a little awkward. The tests were requested because an accusation was made against her."

"Yes, yes. I'm not here to judge their private life. Could I see the horse? Then I can explain the results and why I would like to carry out a re-test."

Kate led the way to the stable. Simon sidled up to her and whispered, "Well handled. You sounded very professional and forthright."

Kate whispered back, "It would help if you kept your head in the game rather than being distracted by every pretty face you see."

Tammy rubbed the horse's forehead, before picking up the headcollar dropped by the door and cautiously entered the stable. "What a transformation from my previous visit!"

Kate and Simon looked over the stable door at Paddy quietly

munching hay. Kate said, "He's been like that since we've been here. Our client, Cynthia, referred to him as a gentle schoolmaster and I found him easy to catch and lead in this morning."

"When did you arrive, and have you had any previous contact with the horse?"

"We arrived yesterday afternoon, and that was the first time we saw the horse," Kate replied, watching the vet take two vials of blood from the horse's neck. Next, the vet took a swab from the horse's mouth, and finally, she cut a small chunk of hair from the mane.

Tammy slid the headcollar off. "I'm taking these to my car. Would either of you two be happy to trot the horse up for me and then lunge it?"

"Sure," Kate replied, following her across the yard. "If one, you tell us why and two, I can find a lunge line."

Securing the test samples in the boot of her car, Tammy said, "We had some odd results back the first time. The horse had high levels of PCP in his bloodstream. Or Phencyclidine, to give its full name, along with something else we haven't been able to identify yet. Normally, the presence of PCP would suggest the horse had been recently sedated. That doesn't appear to be the case here, although I do need to check with Alicia that she hadn't given it a calmer of any description before I arrived last time."

"I'm relatively sure she didn't," Kate said. "She gave us the impression the horse had terrified her so much she didn't even remove the saddle."

"That ties in with what I thought," Tammy replied.

"PCP? Is that the same as Angel Dust?" Simon asked.

"I believe that's one of its street names. It was used as a surgical anaesthetic in the fifties but was quickly withdrawn from use when patients reported experiencing hallucinations and irrational thinking." After shutting the boot of the car, Tammy continued, "The horse seems quiet in the stable, but I would like to see how it reacts to being worked. Assuming it remains relaxed under pressure, I can compare the two sets of samples."

"There's probably a lunge line in the tack shed," Simon said, heading toward the door at the far end of the stable block. He reappeared moments later, holding up a lunge line and whip.

Kate prepared Paddy and led him to the small sand schooling area. She patted and chatted to him in a low voice as they walked to calm her nerves. Paddy had given her no reason to be concerned, but over the years, horses had taught her never to be overly confident, especially when there was an audience. She needn't have worried. Paddy was obedient. If anything, he was on the lazy side, and she had to chase after him to encourage him to canter.

Once Paddy was returned to the stable, Tammy said, "I'll give a final report when I hear back from the lab, but in my opinion, that horse was given something on the day of the accident to make him behave the way he did. I saw the state he was in afterwards with my own eyes."

"How quickly would this drug concoction cause a reaction?" Kate asked. "Alicia tacked the horse up for her husband, and we understand the horse remained calm until about ten minutes later."

Tammy shrugged. "I've no previous experience of a horse being drugged in this way, or what was mixed with the PCP. Generally, when we administer drugs, we're trying to either eliminate pain or calm animals for treatment. I honestly couldn't say how the drug has been given or how quickly it would have had an effect. I don't even know how you could find out. To the best of my knowledge, there haven't been any trials on this sort of thing."

"What ways could the drug have been given?" Kate asked.

Climbing into the driver seat, Tammy said, "The most obvious would be by injection, or via a treat like a sugar lump or rubbed into the horse's gums. I'll ring you once all the results are in."

Simon walked alongside Kate as she returned Paddy to the field. In the gateway, the horse gave a low nicker to the two ponies and sauntered off in their general direction. Watching Kate tie the head collar to the gatepost, Simon said, "So, the horse was drugged. The question is, who by? And was it the same person responsible for the dead crows and glueing the gate?"

Kate turned to face him with her hands on her hips. "No. The question is, why haven't they contacted the police?"

"Until they do, I've got an idea."

"Oh, dear!"

Simon pulled his phone out. "I'm going to ring the driver who called the ambulance." Squinting at the card Alicia had given him the previous evening, he added, "Mark."

"Hang on!" Kate said, trying to stop him from making the call. "Cynthia wanted us to help clear her name. She asked us to be here when the blood tests came in. Our job is done. She didn't say anything about finding out what really happened."

"Don't you want to know?" Before Kate had a chance to reply, Simon held out the phone, and with a grin, said, "Too late. It's ringing."

# CHAPTER NINE

Half an hour later, Simon and Kate pulled up outside a row of terraced cottages in the nearby village of Somerbus. Mark Oates lived in a terraced stone cottage on the edge of the village. Simon pulled in as tight as he could to park on the narrow, steep lane in front of Lilac Cottage. Apprehensively, they squeezed into the narrow gap between the parked car and the cottage to knock on the front door. They didn't have to wait long before the door was opened by a slight man, they judged to be in his late fifties or early sixties. His white, curly hair was neatly trimmed, as was his goatee beard. The few coloured hairs remaining in his bushy eyebrows suggested he was once ginger-haired. His face was dominated by a large, hooked nose. His brown eyes were calm and full of kindness. He waved them in with the eyeglasses he held in his hand and a broad smile. "Come in. Come in. You must be Simon and Kate?"

Simon hesitated. Looking back at his car, he asked, "Am I okay parked there?"

Mark looked over his shoulder at the car. "Yup. That's where I normally park. Mine's in the garage for a service."

Mark led them through a large living room dominated by a fireplace so large it made the wood-burning stove look lost. Catching Kate's reaction, he said, "It's a beauty, isn't it?" Changing direction to walk toward the hearth, he pointed out four large compartments built into the stonework. "What do you think these are?"

Kate moved forward to inspect them with a blank look on her face.

"Bread ovens," Simon said. "Guessing from their size, this was once the village bakery."

With a disappointed look on his face, Mark said, "Correct. We only moved in a few months ago, so I'm still trying to find out a bit more about the history of the place. I'm hoping to find some old photographs of them in use." Mark turned from the fireplace. "Come on, that's not why you're here." He led them through a small dining room and into a large welcoming kitchen. An elderly-looking terrier watched them suspiciously from a basket on the floor. The solid oak table was covered with paperwork, and two laptops faced the carver chair set at the head of the table. "Coffee?"

"Yes, please," Kate and Simon replied.

Busying himself collecting mugs, Mark called over his shoulder, "Move some stuff off the table and sit down. Or if you prefer, go on out to the patio. It's a lovely day. Go and get some fresh air, my mother always used to say. In London, that's a contradiction in terms, I'm afraid."

Kate took the two steep steps up to the back door and opened it. Outside was a comfortable collection of garden furniture set under a wooden trellis covered by a rambling rose. Simon followed her out and settled himself at the table. From the patio, five stone steps led to a steeply terraced garden filled with colourful wildflowers. Kate could just make out a small gateway in the back wall.

Mark joined them, carrying a cafetière, cream jug, homemade biscuits and mugs on a tray. "Please help yourself. If you don't eat them, I'll scoff the lot and have to run it off."

"When did you move here from London?" Simon asked, between mouthfuls of biscuits. "Tell your wife, these are delicious."

"We were born and bred in London. Like thousands of others, we always dreamed about moving to the countryside in search of a healthier lifestyle. Been here about three months, now."

"Did you know Richard or Alicia before the accident?" Kate asked.

"I think I may have passed them in the lanes before, but not to speak to. I got a good price for our old house, but I'm not sure we would be in their social circle if you know what I mean."

"So, you do know something about them?" Kate said.

"I know they live in the old mill house. And clearly, they have horses. This is a beautiful cottage with a charming history and gardens, but it's not in the same league," Mark said, with a hint of jealousy.

Recognising the unattractive sentiment that she shared, Kate was keen to move on. "Tell us what happened the day of Richard's accident?"

"Not a lot to say, really," Mark said, making a great show of recollecting the sequence of events. "When I came around the corner, Richard was lying in the road. The horse was standing up on its back legs and kind of boxing with his front feet. The things where the rider put their feet were flying around all over the place. The horse slipped and fell onto its side. For one terrible moment, I thought it was going to roll over the top of Richard. It scrabbled to its feet and charged off along the lane. That's when I got out of my car and ran to see if I could help."

"You stayed in your car until then?" Kate asked.

"Good God, yes! I know nothing about horses, and I had no intention of going anywhere near the crazy thing. Before it decided to run away in the opposite direction, I was thinking of reversing my car farther away from it."

"Before you came across the scene, did you pass any other vehicles or see anything else that might have frightened the horse?" Kate asked.

"That horse didn't look frightened to me. It looked angry and mean. I stayed in my car because I thought it might attack me if I got out."

"But did you see anyone else around? A car speeding away?" Kate persisted.

"Nope," Mark said, shaking his head. "I didn't pass any vehicles. Oh! There was a man in the adjacent field walking his dogs. I called to him from the gateway, but he didn't hear me. He carried on walking with his head down."

"How far away was he?" Kate asked.

"In my opinion, close enough to have heard me shout for help. Considering the direction, he was walking, he must have seen what happened. I thought it strange and exceedingly rude of him. I guess some people take keeping to themselves, to a whole new level. I thought that attitude was only prevalent in London, while in the countryside, people were always keen to help each other. I did wonder if he was even more scared of horses than I am. But even so."

Simon leaned forward, brimming with excitement. "Could you describe him?"

"Not really. I only saw his back as he walked away. He was walking quickly and looked hunched over. As if he didn't want to be seen."

"Was he tall? Fat? Thin?" Kate asked.

"I'd say he was tallish and strongly built. Not fat. Just stocky. He was wearing what they all wear. Wellingtons, a jacket and a cloth cap. His body language made it obvious he didn't want to help, so I didn't waste any more time on him. I ran over to Richard and checked he was breathing. He was already pretty much in the recovery position, so I didn't make any attempt to move him. I telephoned for an ambulance and stayed by his side until they arrived. Talking nonsense, no doubt. Then his wife and the ambulance arrived and took over. That's about all I can say. Gave me one hell of a shock, I can tell you."

"You've been extremely helpful," Kate reassured him. "Did you tell the police about the man in the field?"

"I'm not sure whether I did or not. They were rather brusque to tell you the truth. When I said I didn't witness what happened, they lost interest in me. They took my details and said they would be in contact, but I've not heard anything since. Not until you called. Do you think I should ring them?"

"Yes, I think you should. Today, if possible," Kate replied.

"Would you like more coffee?" Mark asked.

Simon said, "I think we're good to go." Looking at Kate, he asked,

"Aren't we?"

Kate shook her head before turning her attention back to Mark. "Just a few more questions, if you don't mind? What do you do for a living?"

"I'm a freelance architect."

Kate said, "Ah! That explains why you're at home or driving about during normal work hours."

"I'm not sure there's any such thing as normal work hours these days. But yes, I work from home, so I'm either here or visiting clients or building sites." Mark checked his wristwatch. "I do have an appointment shortly. Have you completed your questions?"

Walking back through the house, Kate noticed the collection of family photographs on the side dresser in the living room. "Is this your wife and son?"

Mark picked up the photograph Kate was referring to. He examined it before saying, "Yes. It was the last photograph of us all together. We lost our son a while back."

"I'm so sorry," Kate said.

"You weren't to know. In many ways, his death was the catalyst for the move out of London. When something like that happens, it changes your perspective. Well, everything, really." Mark returned the photograph to its position. "I needed a change of scenery."

"Could I ask what happened?" Simon said, tentatively.

"Drugs," Mark replied, with a heavy sigh. "He had a good job which paid for a beautiful home and lifestyle. Initially, the drugs were recreational. Weekends only. But things quickly spiralled downwards from there. He lost his job, his home and his so-called friends. All he had left were the drugs. And they killed him."

Kate glared at Simon and repeated to Mark how sorry she was.

Mark patted her on the arm and gave her a sad smile. "It's okay. He's on my mind all the time whether he's spoken about or not."

Once they were back on the road, heading back to Clenchers Mill, Simon whistled. "That information, along with this morning's little gift at the gate, puts things in a whole different light. We need to find that person walking in the field." He tapped his phone, which he'd placed on the dashboard before driving away. "I think I got everything recorded. We can listen to it again when we get back and make notes."

"Simon! That's illegal! You can't go around taping conversations without asking. It's an invasion of privacy."

"Why? He's not a suspect or anything. At least, I don't think he is. He was happy to talk to us. What's wrong with recording it?"

"Everything. You should have at least asked him for permission. Tell me, you at least switched it off when he was talking about his son. That was highly personal."

"I'm not sure. It was still running, but I was some distance away. It may not have picked up anything," Simon said, dismissing Kate's objections.

"You'll have to destroy it, now."

"Don't be so melodramatic. It's only a memory aid. I'm not planning on producing it in a court of law as exhibit A," Simon replied.

"It still feels wrong. You should have said you were recording the conversation."

"In the future, I promise I'll ask for permission. But for now, do you want to listen to it? Or shall I put some music on?"

"Go on, then," Kate finally replied, leaning across to pick up the phone. "But next time, some warning would be good. Before we listen to it, there's something else I need to tell you."

"Go on."

"I didn't want to put any suggestions in Mark's head, so I didn't say anything, back there. The woman I met, Sue, on my run yesterday? She was coming from a field near where I'm guessing Richard fell. It could be the same field as where Mark saw the mystery dog walker."

# CHAPTER TEN

Driving along the private drive, they saw Alicia's car parked in front of the main house. "When do you want to speak to them about what we've discovered today?" Kate asked.

Simon checked the car clock. "I guess we should give them some privacy for now."

"Okay, but we can't put it off forever. The police aren't going to be happy about the long delay in reporting the vandalism of the gate."

"The police may not be overly interested. We need to find out if they have upset local people by making any changes to the use of their land. Rural people can be odd about what they consider to be traditional rights of way. Also, whether they've blocked access to the local hunt. Arguments for and against hunting and shooting get heated on both sides and the police aren't keen to play piggy-in-the-middle."

"Even when there's injury and damage to property?"

Simon stepped out of the car and gave a noncommittal shrug.

Joining him at the front door, Kate said, "I'll make some sandwiches, and then we'll pop over to see them."

"As Richard has just returned from hospital, he'll probably be tired. He may even be sleeping. It might be best to say we've found out a few things we'd like to discuss with them at an agreed time that would suit them."

"I appreciate you're trying to be courteous and all that, but they have a right to know about how the gate was vandalised," Kate said. "If these things have been going on for a while, they won't be terribly shocked about it. It could be things are escalating, and being forewarned is being forearmed and all that. It might persuade them that the time has come to speak to the police."

"Fair point," Simon conceded. "We'll play it by ear when we go over. Alicia might know where Sue lives, and we could visit her later. What do you want to do this evening?"

"We could try the pub in the village for our evening meal. We passed it on the way here. The Wind Whistle Inn."

"We might find out something about what's going on from the locals," Simon said, hopefully.

Alicia opened the front door to them with red, puffy eyes. Simon and Kate asked simultaneously, "Is everything okay? Has something happened?"

With a weak smile, Alicia replied, "Sorry, everything is fine."

"It doesn't look it," Simon said, with concern. Hesitantly, he added, "We saw the vet this morning, and a couple of other things have cropped up. We wondered if this was a good time to talk with you and Richard?"

"Could we do it tomorrow?" Alicia asked.

"Yes, sure," Simon replied.

Before Alicia could close the door, Kate said, "There are some things we think you should be aware of now. It would only take a couple of minutes."

Simon shot her a glare, while Alicia replied, "This really isn't a good time."

Kate stood her ground. "It's obvious that something is very wrong, and we think the police should be told about what's been going on."

Alicia's eyes shot open. "No police! Promise me, no police." When Simon nodded his agreement, Alicia said, in a tired voice, "I'll see you tomorrow," before closing the door.

"What the hell!" Kate said. "Why's she so scared of the police becoming involved?"

"I've no idea but forcing our way in there wasn't going to help,"

Simon replied. "Maybe she'll tell us tomorrow."

◆ ◆ ◆

The twenty-minute walk to the pub was pleasant if uninspiring as high banks on either side of the one-track, potholed lane blocked any possible views as they completed the steep climb. Having discussed Alicia's reaction and argued over whether they should contact the police anyway, they'd agreed to call a truce on the subject for the evening.

"At least it will be downhill on the way home," Simon said cheerfully."

"Not a single vehicle has passed us," Kate said, as the pub and a small cluster of cottages came into sight. "I hope it's open."

"Lovely and peaceful, isn't it? Mind you," Simon said, turning back the way they had come. "If we hear a car approaching around one of those bends on the way home, we will have to jump up onto the banks swiftly. There isn't a lot of passing space."

"True. But I was thinking about Mark Oates. I take it, that's an okay subject. As long as I don't call the police."

"You know my opinion. I think we need to discover why Alicia is reluctant, before taking it upon ourselves, to call the police. That doesn't stop us from trying to find out what's been going on via other means."

"So, where was Mark driving to that day? We're in the middle of nowhere, here. I forgot to ask him," Kate said.

"Ring and ask him tomorrow. I expect the more of this we do, the better we'll get. We'll learn all the important questions we should ask."

Kate chose to ignore the 'more' and 'we' comment. Instead, she nodded towards the thatched, low, two-storey building. The thatch roof came down in curving waves, so, the upstairs windows poked out of the thatch rather than the whitewashed stone wall. "Very quaint, and it looks open. Although, I expect the roof is a terrible fire hazard and full of rats."

Simon nudged her in the ribs. "Do you know what I like about you? You're so romantic."

Kate shoved him back. "You're so hopeless that being around you forces out my practical side."

"Talking of practical, I'm starving," Simon replied, leading the way through a small, white gate and past a collection of wooden tables and chairs painted a jaunty blue. Before opening the door into the lobby, he added, "It's a lovely evening. I wouldn't mind sitting out here and watching the world go by after we've eaten. You can count the number of cars that drive past."

Kate laughed. Flicking the back of Simon's head, she said, "I'm not that pedantic. You're the one going around recording conversations."

Her laugh died away as they entered the dark, wood-panelled building, and the bar chatter ceased. There were only a handful of customers, but she felt as though a hundred, unfriendly eyes were inspecting her. She kept her head down as she followed Simon to the cramped bar. The young girl behind the bar gave a brief, false smile as she poured their drinks. She curtly informed them the restaurant was only open weekends, but they did serve the few bar snacks listed on the chalkboard.

Simon quickly ordered burgers and fries and moved through the gloom to find a table. The pub was a honeycomb of tiny rooms, most only big enough to cram a few small tables into. They settled on a small room with an old-fashioned Aga on one wall. It had a wide window that opened out onto the lane, making the room slightly brighter than some of the others they'd wandered through. The prints on the walls were of hunting scenes with heavy, gold-leafed frames. In between the pictures hung hunting horns and coiled whips. Only when seated did Kate notice on the facing wall was a stuffed, snarling fox with yellow teeth wearing a pair of sunglasses. Next to it was a boar's head wearing a colourful Mexican sombrero.

Following her line of sight, Simon said, "Do you want to move?"

Daunted by the sense of hidden eyes everywhere watching them, Kate shook her head. "It's fine."

"It shows a certain sense of humour, I suppose," Simon said.

"A lack of taste, more like. Especially where people are eating." Shrugging, Kate added, "I needn't look at them." Even as she said it, she felt the macabre draw of the stuffed heads urging her to acknowledge them. She turned in her seat, so she was facing the Welsh dresser covered with plates and copper pans that lined the partition wall. "Not the friendliest of places."

"It's certainly different," Simon agreed. "Hanging around after we've eaten might not be such a good idea after all."

The burgers, when they finally arrived, were bland, but edible. Once they'd eaten, they had a second drink outside, away from the oppressive, depressing atmosphere inside. The outside seating was surprisingly comfortable, and after relaxing in the evening sunshine, they considered staying for another drink.

Their drinks were nearly finished when a dark-haired girl walked out of the pub and sat at the table next to theirs after giving them a cursory glance. The girl tilted her chair back against the wall of the pub and lit up a cigarette. Exhaling smoke, she let her chair drop back to the floor with a heavy thud. She blew smoke in Kate's direction and said, "Are you the ones staying at Clenchers Mill?"

Resisting the automatic urge to cough, Kate smiled at the girl. "We are visiting Richard and Alicia. Do you know them?"

In response, the girl blew a mesmerising smoke ring that curled from her mouth and hung in the air a ridiculously long time. "Are you one of them, then?" Looking Kate up and down, she added, "You look like you are."

Confused, Kate said, "I don't know what you mean. One of them, what?"

The girl blew another smoke ring and watched it float away. "I bet you are."

"Are what?" Kate asked again, becoming annoyed.

The girl angrily stubbed her cigarette out in the clay ashtray. "A bloody anti. Coming out here from town with your high and mighty ideas. Trying to tell us what we should and shouldn't be doing. Clueless. The lot of you."

Kate was about to object when Simon caught her arm. He whispered in her ear, "Leave it. I think she's high."

The girl stood, her chair scratching across the concrete floor. Flicking her wrist, she said, "Hello, gay boy." She stumbled, as she tried to round her table and approach Kate and Simon. She caught her foot on the table leg and fell back onto another chair.

Simon shook his head and whispered to Kate, "Ignore her and she'll go away in a minute. It's not worth causing hassle."

The girl disentangled herself from her table and placed herself in front of Kate.

Face-to-face, Kate could see how enlarged her pupils were in her unfocused eyes. She didn't look old enough to be out of school by herself, let alone stoned outside a pub. Kate moved her chair back a fraction and prepared to spring to her feet if need be.

A tanned, good-looking man in his early twenties with a shock of blond hair, strolled out of the pub. "Jade! There you are. We've been looking for you." His upper-class accent made him sound like he'd stepped out of an old black and white film.

Jade waved her hand in the air. "Hello. You found me." She started a slow handclap. "Congratulations. Clever boy."

The man gave Kate and Simon an apologetic smile before moving toward Jade. He put his arm around her waist and started to lead her back inside the pub. "Come on. Leave these good people alone."

Jade allowed herself to be led away, but as she passed their table, she slurred, "They're not good people. They're antis."

Once they were left alone, Kate said, "Do you think that's connected to things back at the mill?"

"It's possible." Simon rested his chin on his palm, leaving Kate to wonder if he was contemplating the suggestion or falling asleep. Or worse, remembering his jolly capers on the hunting field. His views on blood sports was a conversation they hadn't broached.

After taking a long drink from his pint, Simon said, "Well, we know how they've upset the locals, but I think it's unlikely hunt supporters would go to such lengths to make Richard and Alicia feel unwelcome. Social ostracism is more of their style."

"I could see that upsetting someone like Alicia, but how about Richard? Would a social snub bother him? Maybe, they moved on to direct action when it didn't have the desired effect?"

"When he was married to Cynthia, I remember him being grumpy and un-friendly unless he wanted to charm someone for business reasons. Then, he was positively smarmy. I doubt it would bother him."

"What did he do to make his money?"

"Property developer. I heard he had a reputation for being ruthless. Very involved in the gentrification of rundown city areas, especially in and around London. Buying up old buildings, throwing out the tenants and turning them into expensive, desirable apartments. Cynthia used to be directly involved in the interior design. I'm not sure if she lost interest or was pushed out when Richard decided to employ a professional designer. Alicia. The rest, as they say, is history."

Kate finished her drink, and asked, "Why was that girl so hostile? She would have been a child when hunting was banned. They chase an artificial trail, now, don't they?"

"You're kidding, right?" When Kate continued to look confused, Simon added, "I forgot you're not a country girl. In practical terms, there is no ban. Hunting carries on the same as always. That's why the anti-hunting groups are so active, trying to get film footage and protect the foxes."

"But it's illegal!" Kate said, her eyes wide with surprise. "Why don't the police arrest the huntsmen?"

"Why do you think?"

Before Kate could reply, the blond man from earlier reappeared and placed two pints on their table. "Sorry about earlier. Please accept these as my way to make amends."

"That's very kind of you," Kate replied, still mulling over what Simon had said about hunting. She quickly looked away when she realised, she'd been staring into the stranger's eyes. She couldn't decide whether they were green or brown, but he had the most amazing long eyelashes.

The stranger broke into a heart-stopping grin. "The pleasure is all mine. Please, enjoy. My name is Ben by the way."

"Thank you, Ben," Simon said, breaking the spell Kate had fallen under. "Apology accepted, but maybe you should keep a closer eye on what your girlfriend is up to."

"She's not my girlfriend. I'm yet to find someone as charming as you have. Jade dates my younger brother, Harry. He's got his hands full there," Ben added, pulling a pained expression. "I feel some sense of responsibility for her when I see her out, but I have no control over what she does."

Kate couldn't stop herself from pointing out, "We're just friends."

Ben gave Kate another of his smiles. "Enjoy your stay. Hopefully, we'll bump into each other again before you leave."

Once Ben had returned inside, Simon gave Kate a quizzical look and in an effeminate voice said, "Oh! We're just friends."

# CHAPTER ELEVEN

Kate completed her morning run without incident. Her 'if only' tattoo intensified and mixed with guilt after her surprise attraction to Ben the previous evening. She had no intention of trying to take it any further, but it was the first time she'd felt anything towards a man. Simon had made a move on her shortly after they met. Her furious reaction ensured it would never be repeated.

Her footfalls speeded up to keep in time. If only, if only. She'd be living a different life with Andrew. She would never have met Simon or Ben. She was convinced Andrew wouldn't have gotten along with either of them.

She diverted from her intended return route to Clencher Mill, to run past the horses' paddock and stable block. The horses raised their heads from their contented grazing to watch her pass. Entering the stable yard, she spotted a dark-haired teenager sitting on an upturned bucket. She slowed to a walk and pushed her sweaty hair away from her face. "Hello?"

The dark eyes and delicate features gave the girl's identity away. The smile was absent, but the anxious look was the same. "You must be Alicia's daughter, Helen. I thought you were staying with friends for another week?"

"Clearly, I've returned home," Helen replied, abruptly. "Who are you?"

Avoiding mentioning her connection to Richard's first wife, Kate replied, "I'm Kate. I'm here about your stepfather's riding accident."

Helen stood and picked up the bucket. "*She* sent you."

Stiffening at the rebuke and hearing the anger in the girl's voice, Kate hesitated, unsure of how to reply. The telltale, red splotches left by tears on her face suggested she was upset rather than angry. "Are you, okay?"

"Absolutely fantastic," Helen replied, before stomping away towards the main house.

Kate stared after her, wondering why she was upset and what had caused her to return home earlier than planned. She hoped Richard hadn't taken a turn for the worse. Checking the time, she would have to rush to fit in a shower before their meeting with Alicia and Richard. Presumably, all would be revealed then and speculating beforehand would only waste time. She jogged the short distance to the holiday cottage, kicked off her trainers in the porch and raced up to the bathroom.

Simon called up to her from the bottom of the stairs. "Any surprises on your run today?"

Grabbing a pair of jeans and a clean T-shirt from her room, Kate shouted back down the stairs, "Nothing on the scale of yesterday, but Helen, Alicia's daughter, is here."

"Alicia said she was staying all week with friends," Simon shouted back.

"That's what I thought, but apparently not. She looked upset about something. I'll be down in ten minutes," Kate shouted, before closing the bathroom door.

Feeling refreshed and smelling a lot better, Kate entered the kitchen. "Have I time for a quick coffee?" She stopped and stood open-mouthed when she caught sight of Simon. "What the hell?"

Simon, who appeared to be naked underneath the apron he wore, gave her a mischievous grin. "I thought I would surprise you."

Shaking her head in disbelief, Kate said, "You've certainly done that." She tried to edge around him to the breakfast counter without looking at him.

Simon turned around with her. "Are you trying to take a sneaky peek at my behind?"

Blushing, Kate replied, "Of course not. What are you doing,

anyway?"

"I thought women fantasised about naked chefs."

Edging past, Kate replied, "I think you've been spending too much time on Facebook again."

She'd nearly made it past Simon, when he spun around, showing her his back and he burst out laughing. Underneath the apron, he was wearing a perfectly respectable pair of shorts. "You should have seen your face."

Picking up a dishcloth from the counter, with a relieved smile, Kate swiped at his behind. "You're such an idiot. This isn't the time to be fooling about with everything going on over the way."

"I disagree. It's times like this that people need to keep their sense of humour and spirits up." He pulled off the apron and put on the T-shirt he'd hidden on one of the kitchen chairs. "I had you going, though. Didn't I? You really thought I had nothing on."

Sighing, Kate said, "Do you want a coffee?"

"Sure," Simon replied, slipping onto a chair in front of his open laptop on the kitchen table.

Making two coffees and popping bread in the toaster, Kate asked, "What are you looking at?"

"You were wrong. I don't need any qualifications to become a P.I. I can simply be one."

"You must have to register somewhere? How about insurance if it all goes wrong?"

"Nope. The system is completely unregulated in England." Tilting his chair back until it rested against the wall, Simon added, "Insurance would be a good idea. I can register with different agencies if I want, but it's not compulsory."

Kate carried the coffees and toast to the table. Sitting down, she took a mouthful of toast. "You're really keen on the idea, then?"

"Oh, yes. After we've spoken to Alicia and Richard, I'm going to telephone Mark Oates to discover what he was doing out on these lanes and visit your mysterious walker, Sue." Shutting the laptop lid, he took a slurp of his coffee. "I looked at Richard's property development company while you were out running. He's still the Managing Director, and the website says he continues to play an active role."

Kate thought back to her conversation with Cynthia. "It could be he told Cynthia he is retired for financial reasons."

The front legs of Simon's chair hit the floor with a thud. He grabbed the notepad next to the laptop and started writing. "You're a natural at this. I'll make a note of that."

Kate shook her head as she finished her toast. Checking the clock, she said, "Come on, Sherlock or we might miss them."

Simon stood and slipped the notepad into the back pocket of his shorts. With a grin, he said, "Does that make you, my Watson?"

"It doesn't make me, your anything. When we have the second set of results from the vet, we should call Cynthia. If you ask her nicely, she might write you a testimonial for your website."

"What website?"

Walking to the door, Kate replied, "The one you're going to need so people can contact you. You know you'll end up following husbands suspected of having affairs or if you're really lucky, delivering summonses for a firm of solicitors."

Closing the front door behind them, Simon said, "I'll be choosey about which cases we take on. And I believe in creating opportunities, which is why I'm going to offer our services to Alicia and Richard. We're going to find out who left those crows by the gate and drugged their horse."

"Fine, but it's the 'we' that's concerning me," Kate replied, dryly.

"We need a name for the company. How about The Black Crow Investigates?"

Kate couldn't stop herself from laughing uncontrollably. "Sorry, sorry," she repeated when she could. With tears of laughter running down her face, she said, "No. It sounds stupid and suggests you're dark and dangerous when you're neither."

With mock offence, Simon struck a pose and replied, "I could be dark, dangerous and mysterious if I wanted to be."

Between bouts of hysterical laughter, Kate said, "You're more of a white pony than a black horse."

# CHAPTER TWELVE

Arriving at the main house, they found the front door open. Kate stopped Simon from wandering in unannounced and rang the doorbell.

"Come on in. It's open. We're in the living room," Alicia called out.

Simon gave Kate a smug, 'I told you so' look, before leading the way. Alicia greeted them in the doorway and whispered, "I'm sorry about yesterday. Things rather got on top of me." Guiding them through the hallway, she said, "He is rather groggy and becomes irritated when he can't remember things." She moved quickly to her husband's side to introduce them.

Richard grunted from his sprawled-out position on one of the sofas. He grimaced as he sat up. Alicia fussed over him, moving cushions to support his back before seating herself on a nearby armchair.

"You'll have to excuse me not getting up," Richard said. "How is Cynthia and the great and good of the old area generally?"

Kate observed as Simon filled him in on local gossip. Her first impression of Richard was not favourable. He hadn't even thanked Alicia for trying to make him comfortable. He reminded her of a spoilt child, expecting to be waited on hand and foot. Despite looking pale and drawn, he was a naturally handsome man, but he had the look of vanity about him. His black hair, lightly peppered with grey, was neatly styled, and he was freshly shaven. His pale blue pyjamas were monogrammed, and his tartan dressing gown and slippers matched. One arm was in a sling, but poking out from the other sleeve of his dressing gown was a chunky, gold watch. A copy of the Financial

Times sat in easy reach on the small coffee table. To his side, a single crutch balanced on the arm of the sofa.

"Can I get you something to eat or drink?" Alicia asked.

Kate declined, and the conversation between Simon and Richard stuttered to a halt.

"No, thank you. We had breakfast before coming over here. We wanted to talk to you about the vet's findings and something else," Simon said.

Silence fell, and all eyes turned towards Helen, who walked in and plonked herself down on an armchair. "What? I can't listen in?" Helen said, aggressively. "Aren't I a part of the family as well?"

"Of course you are, dear," Alicia said, in her gentle sing-song voice. "This is just about Richard's accident."

"Haven't you got any homework to do?" Richard suggested.

Ignoring Richard, Helen replied to her mother, "You said this was my home, and I want to know what's going on. You can't send me away every time things get difficult. I'm fourteen years old. I'm not a baby anymore."

"You're welcome to stay. I didn't think you'd be that interested, is all," Alicia replied.

Kate watched the interaction with interest. She was amazed at how quickly the façade of a perfect life had fallen away, and she almost felt sorry for Alicia. Her eyes still looked puffy, with dark rings under them, and she appeared more anxious than yesterday.

Keeping his focus on Richard, with only occasional glances towards Alicia, Simon said, "The vet has confirmed they found traces of a drug similar to PCP in the horse's bloodstream. The drug was used in the past as a sedative. As a street drug, it is taken to cause hallucinations and a feeling of detachment from reality. When the vet came back yesterday, she repeated the tests when the horse was calm and relaxed for comparison. We're hoping to hear back from her today with those results. The implications are obvious." Looking directly at Richard, he asked, "Who would want to see you seriously injured, if not dead?"

Richard shared a worried look with Alicia, before replying, "I've no idea. Is it possible the horse picked up something accidentally? We keep our meadows in a natural state. We don't spray, at all. A lot of wild plants have attributes we don't fully appreciate yet. The horse could have reacted to a wild herb."

"Unlikely, I would have thought," Simon said.

"But it is worth checking that possibility with the vet," Kate said.

After an awkward silence, Simon said, "There's something else."

"Go on," Richard said, warily. "Spit it out. There's obviously something else you want to tell me."

"Yesterday morning, Kate went for an early run. She found your gate had been glued shut and two dead crows tied to the tree next to it."

Helen leapt up from her seat and ran out of the room without saying anything.

Kate half rose from her chair and asked, "Should I go after her?"

The colour drained from Alicia's face, and she nervously played with the hem of her shirt. "Leave her for now. I'll go and find her later." Looking toward Richard, slowly shaking her head, she said, "I didn't see anything when I left for the hospital."

"Because we removed the glue and cut down the birds." Simon looked first at Alicia and then at Richard. "What's going on, here?"

Alicia and Richard had a silent conversation with their eyes and facial expressions. Richard finally said, "We've upset the local field sports set by banning hunting and shooting on our land. I've never been a fan of blood sports, and Alicia feels very strongly about it. I believe Alicia told you of her plans to turn this place into a retreat for writers and artists. Anyone really, who wants to escape the hustle and bustle for a while and feel close to nature. We want to create a feeling of tranquillity here, and we don't need the tweed brigade with their fancy socks marching through here with their guns. The gate and the dead birds would be their way of expressing their opinion."

"You don't sound very concerned? Are you going to report it to the police?" Kate asked.

"And add more salt to the wound? No. They've had their fun. Reporting them will only cause more grief," Richard replied. "Once the hunting season starts in a couple of months, they'll all be too busy to set up any more pranks."

"There's something else that makes me believe you should be taking things more seriously," Simon said. "We spoke to Mark yesterday. The gentleman who called the emergency services after your accident. He saw somebody walking across the fields, away from where it happened. He described the person as someone from the country set. The tweed brigade, as you call them. What if that person gave something to your horse to make it act the way it did?"

"I'm not sure how, but they'd be damn fools if they did. The doctors say my memory should slowly return. If someone stopped me in the lane and did something to the horse, I'll remember it in time," Richard said.

Alicia's already pale, pinched face turned ashen.

Kate said, "You could have been killed. If the person thinks you will be able to recognise them, they might come back for you."

The slow realisation knocked the calm confidence from Richard's face. He slumped back on the sofa. Alicia's previous anxious look had turned to one of terror.

"I think we should reconsider contacting the police," Richard said.

Alicia pulled her hands away and sat back. "No police. You promised."

Visibly shaken, Richard said, "Could you fix me a brandy? I need to think."

"Should you be drinking in your condition?" Alicia said with a concerned frown."

"A drink is exactly what I need in my condition." Watching Alicia pour his drink, Richard asked, "What is it you two do, again?"

"We're private investigators," Simon proudly announced.

"Do you have a name?"

"Oh, yes. The White Horse Investigators," Simon said, to a roll of Kate's eyes. "I'm afraid I didn't think to bring my business cards with me."

"A word of advice from one businessman to another. Always come prepared," Richard said.

"Advice taken," Simon replied, nodding his head. "Does that mean we're hired?"

"I think you need to contact the police," Kate said, casting Simon a warning look.

"I think involving the police may make matters worse," Richard said, looking at Alicia. "Discreet enquiries would be preferable in the circumstances."

"We can be discreet," Simon said, looking hopeful.

Richard reached forward to shake Simon's hand. "Make sure you're damned discreet."

"Will do. Oh! There's one other thing, Alicia. Do you know where your friend Sue lives?"

Alicia shook her head. "I've no idea."

"Alicia's little stalker? What's she got to do with anything?" Richard asked.

"Possibly, nothing. We wondered if she saw something in the lane around the time of your accident. Why do you call her a stalker?"

"She's taken a right shine to Alicia, hasn't she? Always popping up when you least expect it, offering to help."

"She's from the village, then? You didn't know her before?" Kate asked.

When Alicia didn't say anything, Richard prompted her, "You said you'd seen her somewhere before, didn't you?"

Alicia quietly replied, "I said she looked like someone I'd seen before in London." Handing Richard his drink, she retook her seat next to him. "It couldn't be the same person. She's probably no more than your typical nosey villager with too much time on her hands. I wouldn't read too much into it."

Richard put his arm around her shoulder and said, "Why don't we let these two be the judge of that?"

"Do you know her full name and where she lives?" Kate asked.

"Sue Evans," Richard replied. "I think she lives at the far end of the village. There's a row of terraced cottages before you leave the village. I've seen her entering the one at the end."

"Thank you for your help. We'll make a start, and I'll pop around later with a contract and a note of our fees," Simon said, preparing to leave.

# CHAPTER THIRTEEN

Closing the front door behind them, Kate and Simon were surprised to see Mark Oates climbing from his car.

"What are you doing here?" Kate asked. "You said you didn't know Richard and Alicia?"

"I don't," Mark replied, turning to retrieve something from the back seat of his car. He turned, holding an enormous bouquet of flowers. "I couldn't sleep last night thinking about the dreadful experience they've been through." He thrust the bouquet into Simon's hands. "I decided to bring these. Not much I know, but I thought the gesture might help."

"They're beautiful. I'm sure they'll be very appreciative," Kate said, moving aside to give him access to the front door.

"Umm. I was going to leave the flowers on the front step for them to find later. I thought it would be a pleasant surprise for them."

"Don't be silly. I'm sure they would like to thank you personally," Kate said.

"I'm in a bit of a rush. You take them in for me," Mark replied, backing away to his car. He started the engine, but Simon prevented him from driving forward by placing his free hand on the side of the bonnet. Mark lowered the window, irritation bubbling beneath his smile. "Yes?"

Simon moved to the car door. Giving his best Columbo impersonation, he said, "There's one thing bothering me. What were you doing on the lane at the time of the accident? It's rather out of the way."

"A bit embarrassing, really," Mark replied. "The damn sat nav is broken, and I became lost returning from a project visit over

Yatton way. I saw the sign on the main road for the Wind Whistle Inn. I ate in there several times when looking for a property to buy in the area. I felt sure I would be able to find my way from there. Can I go now? I'm going to be late."

Simon stepped back from the car. "Of course." He watched the car disappear along the driveway and read out the card attached to the bouquet. "I hope you feel better soon. Mark." Turning to face Kate, he said, "I'll take these in and see you back at the cottage."

"What? Oh, yes," Kate said. "I was just wondering what sort of reception he received at the pub."

"I guess he never crossed paths with Jade," Simon replied. "It may be a different place on weekends."

Doubting the pub's atmosphere could change that much, Kate decided to take the longer route through the stable yard. Paddy and the two ponies were tied up, and Helen was brushing the coat of the bay pony. She jumped back and dropped the brush when Kate approached. Retrieving the brush, Helen muttered, "You nearly gave me a heart attack, creeping up like that."

"Sorry, I didn't mean to make you jump," Kate said, closing the gap between them. Pointing her thumb over her shoulder in the direction of the main house, she said, "You seemed upset when we mentioned the gate and the crows back there. Are you okay?"

"Would you be if it happened to you?" Helen replied, resuming her brushing. After a couple of strokes, she threw the brush to the floor. "God! I hate this place. I wish we'd never come here."

Kate picked up the brush and started to untangle the tail of the grey pony. "Then, why did you come back from your friend's house early?"

Helen started to say something but appeared to change her mind. She shoved her hands deep into her jeans pocket. Shaking her head, she said, "You wouldn't understand."

"Try me. Were you worried about Richard?"

Helen pulled her hands from her pockets and curled them into fists. "Despite what he likes to think, not everything revolves around him."

"How do you mean?" Startled by the look of guilt on Helen's face, Kate said, "Do you know who was behind that malicious prank at the gate?"

Helen threw her hands out to the side before marching away. She shouted back, "Leave me alone!" and broke into a run.

"What should I do with the horses?" Kate called after her. Receiving no reply and seeing there were no beds made up in any of the stables, she led them back to their paddock.

In the guest cottage, breakfast things had been tidied away, and Simon was bent over his laptop on the kitchen table. He looked up and said, "There you are. I wondered where you got to."

Moving to the counter to make coffee, Kate replied, "I bumped into Helen on the way back. I'm not sure whether she was being overdramatic, but she said something that suggested she knows more about what is going on here than she is letting on."

"Yeah?" Simon said, keeping his focus on the laptop screen.

"It could be I'm reading too much into things, and she's a typical teenager struggling to adapt to a new home and her mother's relationship with Richard." Kate carried two mugs of coffee to the table and sat at the opposite end to Simon. Blowing across the top of her coffee, she asked him what he was doing.

"I've downloaded a standard P.I. Contract for Richard to sign, and now I'm setting up a website. I thought I should make a start before trying to find Sue's cottage. How about you? What are you planning on doing this morning?"

"Nothing, much. Once the vet contacts us with the second set of results, I'll update Cynthia. After that? I don't know. I might take the dogs for a walk."

"If you walk them along to where Richard had his accident, you could check out the field where Mark said he saw the walker. Find out whether this unknown person could have seen what was going on in the road. It might be because of the hedge the walker was completely oblivious. Especially if he ..."

Kate interrupted him to say, "Or she?"

Simon continued, "Or she was wearing earphones. Alternatively, if they did see everything, why did they choose to walk away?"

"And what about Mark? It could be his sleepless night, and his kind gesture of the flowers was fuelled by guilt. If he was lost, he may have been driving too fast and not paying full attention. Other than the mysterious walker, there's no one to confirm or contradict his version of events."

"Except for the drug tests," Simon said.

The shrill ring of a mobile phone filled the room. Ending the call, Kate said, "That was the vet. The second tests came back nearly normal. Faint traces that there had been drugs in his system. I'll ring Cynthia and let her know the horse had been drugged, so she is in no way responsible for what happened." Patting Simon on the back, Kate added, "Your first mystery is resolved."

"And a new one is just beginning," Simon said, cheerfully. "What do you want to do for supper tonight?"

"I don't fancy a return to the Wind Whistle, that's for sure. At first sight, this area looked so pretty, but there is something wrong about the place. It makes me feel on edge and an unwanted intruder. There's probably a supermarket in the area. I could cook for us."

"There must be other pubs and restaurants. I'll ask Richard and Alicia for a recommendation while I'm over there."

"There's a list of places they recommend in the cottage," Kate said. "I saw it when we arrived. I should have realised there was a reason there was no mention of the Wind Whistle."

While Simon went to the main house to discuss his contract terms and to explain the vet's findings, Kate collected Simon's dogs and set off along the lane. At least the dogs accepted her as she was and didn't view her as an outsider.

The faint scratch marks on the surface where Paddy had played up were already fading. Further along the lane was a sharp, right-hand bend. If Mark was travelling any faster than he claimed, his stopping distance would have put him nearly at the spot where Richard fell. If it wasn't for the vet's findings and Alicia's description of the horse's behaviour hours after the incident, the obvious conclusion was that Mark had spooked the horse.

She wandered over to the gateway. The field was full of sheep, and it wasn't marked as a footpath. It could be the person Mark saw was the owner tending to the sheep. The gate wasn't padlocked. She slipped the dogs' leads on and wandered into the field, looking behind her every few steps. She crisscrossed the field several times. There were only a few spots where someone in the field would have had a clear view of the road. Most of the time, it was obscured by the hedge. Checking the scene hadn't helped one way or the other. She closed the gate behind her and continued her walk along the quiet lane.

Their visit to the end of the village was also a wasted trip as Sue Evans wasn't in. While Kate was scribbling a note to put through the letterbox, the next-door neighbour came out to ask them what they were doing. "She's usually in at this time, but I haven't seen her today. Are you anything to do with the other man who has been trying to get in touch with her?"

"I don't think so," Kate replied. "What did he look like?"

"I didn't take much notice. He was pretty average with grey hair. He said he was an old friend looking her up."

"Then no," Kate said, pushing her note through the letterbox. "We're trying to contact her about a horse-riding accident she might have seen."

# CHAPTER FOURTEEN

The Squirrel Inn was a red-brick building nestled in a valley five miles away from Clenchers Mill. It wasn't so attractive from the outside as the Wind Whistle, but it came highly recommended by Richard and had good reports on Trip Advisor. Kate had checked to avoid a repeat performance of the previous evening. While on the site, she had looked up the Wind Whistle Inn. It had numerous one-star reviews, many written as a personal attack on the pub's support for blood sports.

Once through the entrance, the ugly façade of the pub was forgotten. In front of them was a roomy bar, lined with stools. The stone flooring was slate grey, and the walls were painted eggshell blue. To their left was a doorway and a step down into another room. A sign above the door read, 'Local's bar,' and the muffled sound of chattering and laughter escaped in pulses. To their right was a central stone chimney. The unlit fireplace was decorated with wicker baskets of dried flowers. A large alcove was filled with tables and chairs. At the far end of the airy room, tables were laid up for food.

The girl behind the bar welcomed them with a genuine smile, "Hi, I'm Laura. What would you like to drink?" The long bar offered an extensive selection of real ales. They were encouraged to sit at the bar and try free samples. Simon settled on a pint of Sixpenny Gold. Kate couldn't resist a half-pint of Dorset's Piddle Jimmy Riddle. Laura handed over the food menus, informing them everything was produced locally.

Thanking her, Kate said, "This is a massive improvement on where we ate yesterday."

"Where was that?"

A knowing look spread over Laura's face when Kate replied, "The Wind Whistle Inn."

"Where are you staying?"

"Clenchers Mill. Over in Leighterton. With Alicia and Richard Fielding. They recommended you to us."

"I'll be sure to let my parents know. How is Richard? I heard he had a nasty fall."

"He's back home, now. How do you know them?" Kate asked.

"Only from in here. My parents know them a little better. They're the owners. I'm home from Uni, so of course, I get roped into working behind the bar." Picking up a cloth to wipe the spotless counter, Laura asked, "So, how come you ended up in the Wind Whistle? Didn't Alicia warn you to stay away?"

"It was the nearest and looked lovely from the outside," Kate said. "We're staying in the holiday cottages, not the main house and didn't think to mention where we were going to Alicia."

"Is there bad blood between the Wind Whistle and Alicia?" Simon asked.

"You could say that!" Laura poured herself a glass of lemonade. "The previous owners of Clenchers Mill hosted several fox hunt meets at the house and ran a pheasant shoot once a month during the shooting season. Alicia and Richard put a stop to all that and banned the hunt from crossing their land. The landlady of the Wind Whistle is the niece of the current Hunt Master."

"Ah! That would explain the hostility," Simon said.

"The hunt regularly meets in the Wind Whistle car park, and all the terrier boys, hunt staff and followers drink in there."

"What's your view on hunting?" Kate asked.

"I would rather not say. Most people around here want an easy life and don't care one way or the other. The hunt followers are influential people, but at the same time, the hunt saboteurs are very active in this area. Most people keep their heads down and try not to become involved. Because of recent events, the subject has become even more volatile than usual," Laura said.

"How come?"

"A young boy. Only fifteen committed suicide. He was an avid hunt follower. People are claiming he did it because he was bullied at school because he hunted."

"I can see why that would cause ill-feeling," Simon said.

"It was very sad but …" The girl leaned forward over the bar and quietly said, "I only knew the boy from sight, but I can think of several other reasons why he would be bullied. He was quite odd and very overweight. If you didn't know better, from the way he looked and behaved, you'd assume he was about ten years old. I was shocked when the newspapers reported him being fifteen. I always thought he was much younger."

Two men in suits walked in and took up a couple of stools at the bar. "The usual, Laura. It's been a long day."

Laura hurried to collect fresh pint glasses from beneath the bar. After serving the new customers, she said to Kate and Simon, "Let me know when you're ready to order your food and where you'll be sitting."

The suit nearest them at the bar leaned toward Kate and said, "Go for one of the steaks."

Kate thanked him for the recommendation and followed Simon into the dining area to find a table. The pub rapidly filled up, and they didn't have the chance to speak again to Laura. Their steaks were cooked to perfection, and after sharing an Eton Mess for pudding they could hardly move. They both agreed they'd be returning before they left the area. Reluctantly, Kate accepted they would also return to the Wind Whistle to ask a few questions.

# CHAPTER FIFTEEN

Loud barks coming from the kitchen woke Kate and Simon. They met outside their respective bedroom doors on the upstairs landing.

"They don't normally bark in the night," Simon said, rubbing the sleep from his eyes. "Unless someone is prowling very close."

Tying her dressing gown she had hastily thrown on doubly tight, Kate whispered, "Do you think there's someone in the cottage?"

"I can't hear anyone moving around."

"You can't hear anything over the barking," Kate whispered back. "Have you got anything to use as a weapon?"

Simon raised his hand to show the hairbrush he was carrying.

Looking unimpressed, Kate said, "It might be better to call the police from up here if we think there's someone downstairs."

"If there's anyone nearby, I think they're outside," Simon said. "I'll grab the poker from the fireplace. You grab the torch from the kitchen."

Downstairs, both dogs were barking and scratching at the back door. Simon let them out, and Kate shone the torch in the direction they ran. Hearing nothing, they cautiously followed them out, holding their makeshift weapons in front of them. The dew on the grass quickly turned their bare feet cold and wet as they ran after the dogs. They found them at the front of the main house, intently pacing around Alicia's Range Rover. Glass from the shattered front windscreen glistened in the torchlight. Simon quickly called the dogs back and held them by the collar. "We'll have to go back and get some shoes."

A window above them creaked open, and Richard shouted.

"What's going on out there? My wife is calling the police."

"It's us," Simon called up to the window. "Someone has smashed Alicia's front windscreen. We need to take the dogs back and get ourselves some shoes."

"Hang on." Richard's head disappeared and reappeared as a pair of slippers, and some deck shoes rained down on them. "Did you see who did it?"

"No. The dogs woke us. I think they're long gone, but we'll have a poke about to make sure." Simon dragged the dogs over to Kate. Taking the torch from her, he said, "Hold these while I grab the shoes and take a closer look." He collected the footwear from beneath the window, put on the slippers and threw the deck shoes to Kate. Shining the light into the car, he saw what had been used to smash the window.

He flashed the light on the ground. There was a clear track in the dew leading back towards the drive. There was also a trail leading to the garage. The bottom of the metal door was dented and bent. Simon shone the light in an arc over the front grounds. All was quiet and still. He called up to Richard, "It looks like they attempted to break into the garage but gave up. We'll be able to see more in the morning."

Alicia appeared in the window next to Richard. Tension and fear etched on her face. "Are you sure they've gone?"

Simon looked back at his dogs. "As sure as I can be. If they were still nearby, the dogs would be more agitated. Have you called the police?"

"Not yet. If they've gone, I don't see the point of dragging them out here at this hour," Alicia replied.

"Should we come down?" Richard asked.

"There's nothing more we can do until the morning. If you're not calling the police, we may as well all go back to bed. If anyone comes back, the dogs will alert us," Simon said.

Helen's head appeared at another window. "What's going on?"

"Nothing. Go back to bed," Richard said.

Simon walked away from the house when the three of them started to argue. He whispered to Kate, "Take the dogs back to the house. Someone has left a dead fox on the front passenger seat." Looking up at the closing bedroom windows, he added, "I'll dispose of it now and tell Richard in the morning."

"Okay. But don't throw it away. Put it in the recycling bin with the birds."

Simon returned to the cottage to find Kate in the kitchen, nursing a mug of coffee. "I thought you'd be asleep by now."

Kate looked at him, incredulously. "Do you think I could go back to sleep after that?"

"Drinking coffee isn't going to help. I'm going back to bed for a few hours' sleep." From the doorway, Simon added, "It's three o'clock now. I'll see you at eight."

"Wait! Are you seriously going back to sleep? What if they return and do something worse?"

"The dogs will wake us," Simon replied calmly, before stifling a yawn.

"I don't want to stay here another night. I'm not convinced it's safe," Kate said, her voice higher than usual and tinged with fear.

Sighing, Simon returned to the kitchen cabinet, flicked on the kettle and pulled out a mug from the overhead cupboard. "Do you want another one?"

"Yes, please," Kate replied, holding out her empty mug for him to take. "Don't you think Alicia's reluctance to call the police has gone beyond odd? The intruders could have gone to collect tools to break into the garage and are creeping around out there, now. Alicia will need a police reference to make an insurance claim on the car. And for the garage door. What if the progress from property damage? We could all be murdered in our beds!"

Simon joined her at the table. Rubbing his eyes with the heels of his palms, he said, "Maybe they won't bother putting it through insurance. I don't think money is an issue for them. Or she's tired and would prefer to speak to the police with a clear head after a good night's sleep, in the morning?"

"Do you honestly think they're in the land of nod, snoring their heads off? I expect they are feeling as vulnerable as I do. Probably more so, as this is aimed directly at them, not us."

Struggling to keep his eyes open despite the strong coffee, Simon said, "There's a camping bed in my room that I can sleep on. Why don't you get into my bed or I can drag the camping bed into your room?" Lifting the poker, he'd rested against the table, he added, "I can take this up with us, and we can leave our phones next to the bed. If the dogs bark again, I'll call the police, immediately. We both need to get some sleep if we're going to get to the bottom of this."

Nervously pushing her mug in small circles, Kate replied, "Okay, but I'm serious about not wanting to stay here. They've already drugged a horse. What if they poison the dogs? They could torch the cottage with us trapped inside."

Simon moved over to her. He put one hand on her shoulder and raised Kate's chin. "I won't let anything happen to you or the dogs. They can stay in the bedroom with us tonight. They'll bark just the same if they hear anyone moving about outside. Okay? Let's go to bed. We can talk about everything else in the morning."

Kate nodded and reluctantly followed Simon upstairs. Hesitant at first, the dogs bounded up the stairs when Simon called them and galloped excitedly around the top landing. "Don't get used to it," Simon said sternly. When he opened the bedroom door, both dogs leapt onto the double bed and wagged their tails.

# CHAPTER SIXTEEN

Kate slept fitfully for a few hours. A nightmare scene of the locals from the Wind Whistle Inn carrying torches of fire, marching toward the mill and shouting obscenities woke her up. Drenched in sweat and wedged between the two dogs, her mind raced. Every time she closed her eyes, she had visions of mutilated foxes attacking her. The muffled snoring coming from Simon on the camp bed irritated rather than soothed her.

When Kate tried to push the duvet off, the contented dogs refused to move. The duvet was pinned down on either side of her by their sleeping weight. She started to wriggle her way out of the straight jacket. Feeling trapped, she panicked, kicking out at the duvet until she finally pulled herself free. Shaking, she sat down on the side of the bed. Simon's eyes flickered open and closed again. She collected her clothes and quickly dressed. When she opened the door, the dogs jumped from the bed and danced around her, keen for an early breakfast.

She stifled a scream when she opened the kitchen door. Simon had left his jacket draped over the back of a chair, and in the dim light, it resembled a person. Shaking her head at her silliness, she decided to make proper coffee in the cafetière rather than instant. She gave the dogs their breakfast and watched them wolf it down. Unlike her imagination, they seemed satisfied there wasn't someone lurking in the shadows waiting to kill them when their backs were turned. A cold chill ran down her spine at the thought.

She was adding milk to her coffee when a sudden sound of something being dragged across the floor caused her to drop the milk. The bottle smashed, sending up a spray of milk and fragments of glass. Her heart rate was through the roof. Turning around, annoyed by the unnecessary fright, she shouted, "Stop it! Both of you!" The dogs play fighting, had knocked into the table, shifting it across the floor and that was what had startled her. She unlocked and opened the back door. "Out!" She relocked and bolted the door behind them before clearing up the smashed milk bottle.

She slumped onto a chair to enjoy her coffee. Frantic scratching started up at the door. Feeling guilty, she heaved herself up to open the door. It wasn't the dog's fault that she was exhausted and on edge, and she shouldn't have taken her anxiety out on them. What if intruders had left poisoned meat outside for them? She'd never forgive herself if they died. She opened the door just wide enough for the dogs to squeeze through. They barged through and instantly forgave her. They jumped up at her, battling each other for her attention. Kate pushed them down. "Hang on. Door locked and then cuddles."

The dogs rushed to Simon's side when he appeared, bleary-eyed in the doorway, a few moments later. "Morning. Have the dogs been fed?" When Kate nodded, he bent forwards to jokingly scold the dogs. "You can't fool me. I wasn't born yesterday." Catching sight of the cafetière, he said, "Is there enough for me?"

Joining Kate at the table, he asked, "How are you feeling this morning? Do you still want to leave?"

"A part of me does. Last night spooked me. It wouldn't be so bad if they would call the police. My imagination has been working overtime, trying to figure out why Alicia and Richard are so reluctant. I can only think they have something to hide. I've come up with everything from they're part of a major, drug-smuggling ring to them being people traffickers. None of which makes me feel happy about being here."

"You do look shattered and on edge. What about the other part of you?"

"That part wants to find out who is playing such horrid tricks. But that doesn't stop me from feeling nervous about what might happen, next."

"How about a compromise? One more night and if they haven't called the police and we're no closer to discovering what's going on, we could have a rethink about staying on-site?" Simon gave Kate his best, puppy-dog face. "I don't want to fail on my first case."

"Your first case was proving Cynthia didn't knowingly send a crazy horse to kill her ex-husband. You've done that. And stop making that pathetic face." Carrying the dirty mugs to the sink, Kate said, "I felt safer camping in the van in the middle of nowhere than I do here."

"The pranks aren't being aimed at us. We're quite safe, here." When Kate didn't look convinced, Simon changed the subject. "You're better at this than me. Where do you suggest we start today?"

Kate shook her head. "Flattery won't get you anywhere." Closing the dishwasher door, she said, "First, we have a good look at the damage caused last night and speak to Alicia and Richard about contacting the police. Then, if we can't get hold of Sue Evans, I suggest we find out who owns the sheep in the field next to where the horse freaked. If the owner says it wasn't him in the field, he might know who else walks their dogs there. As far as I could tell, there's no public footpath through the field, and most dog walkers tend to avoid fields with livestock if they can."

"Works for me. You're not going to like this idea, but I think we should stick with our plan to re-visit the Wind Whistle Inn later."

"You're right. I don't like the idea, especially after what happened last night. I think it's highly likely someone in there is responsible for the attacks," Kate replied.

"That's exactly why I think we should go in there. Show we won't be intimidated. I'll go by myself if you prefer?" Simon offered.

"We'll see. Let's make a start by seeing how much damage was caused to Alicia's Range Rover and the garage doors."

Approaching the house, they heard raised voices. Alicia and Helen were arguing by the front door, although they couldn't hear what was being said. Alicia caught sight of them and waved. Helen turned towards them, scowled and marched away in the opposite direction. Over her shoulder, she shouted, "Typical of you to be convinced that everything is about you."

Watching the direction Helen took, Simon said to Kate, "You speak to Alicia. See if you can discover what that was all about. I'll go after Helen."

Alicia wore a forced smile, but the vague dark marks beneath her eyes had turned to black rings. She played with the front door catch as she stared at Simon chasing after her daughter. Nervously fiddling with the catch, she tried to make light of the situation. "Teenagers. Who'd have them? I guess I was naïve to think Helen would be any different. Things were just a little delayed with her. She used to be so sensible and level-headed."

Kate gave a sympathetic smile. Alicia's eyes were red. She couldn't be sure if it was from lack of sleep or crying. Probably a combination of both. "Always a difficult time. What were you arguing about?"

Alicia's slender fingers continued to push the door catch in and out as she stared in the direction Helen and Simon had gone. "She wasn't like this up until a couple of months ago. Now, she's moody and sullen all the time. And that damned phone is never out of her hands. I can see why it annoys Richard. Even when you talk to her, she's checking the screen constantly." Her shoulders slumped, and her hand fell away from the door catch. "Come on in. I'm sorry you had to see that."

Following Alicia to the kitchen, Kate couldn't see any sign of Richard. She settled onto a chair while Alicia poured her a coffee.

Sliding onto an adjacent chair, Alicia said, "We haven't been outside to check the damage, yet. How bad is it?"

"The front windscreen is smashed, and the bottom of the garage door has been damaged. Simon thinks they used a crowbar to try to prise it open."

"Why didn't they try to force the lock? Oh, well. I expect Richard will go out to check it later. He's still snoring his head off. How he can sleep is beyond me. Although maybe the painkillers have something to do with it." Alicia lifted her mug. Coffee spilt over the edge in her trembling hands, and she lowered it to the table. "I didn't sleep a wink last night. I kept thinking they might come back. Was there any other damage?"

Considering the exhaustion and anxiety on Alicia's face, Kate decided not to mention the dead fox. "I think it was just the windscreen and the garage door. It was hard to see in the dark."

Alicia's eyes restlessly darted around the room. "Yes, yes. We ought to check properly before ringing the garage."

"And report it to the police?"

Alicia stared into her coffee mug. "I don't see the need to call them out if it's only the windscreen. I'm sure they have far more important things to do than investigate minor vandalism."

Shocked, Kate said, "You should report it. Someone was prowling around your house …" The sentence died in her throat when she saw the rising fear on Alicia's face. "Well, I guess it's your decision."

Alicia stood and crossed the kitchen. Looking out the kitchen window over the sink with her back to Kate, she said, "I think it's for the best. It will only aggravate them even more."

"Them! You know who it is?"

"Of course, I don't. I meant whoever it is. How dare you accuse me like that!"

Kate finished her coffee in an uncomfortable silence. Alicia collected her empty cup and took it to the sink. "I'm sorry, I snapped. I seem to be doing a lot of that, recently."

"Forget it," Kate replied, "It's understandable in the circumstances. I feel on edge myself, so it must be worse for you. Is that what happened this morning? I couldn't help but overhear Helen claiming you thought everything was all about you?"

Without turning from facing the window, Alicia said, "Unfortunately, I think it is. My views on animal welfare have annoyed people. You know, I used to dream of living somewhere like this when I was a child. I didn't realise the reality would be so … difficult. Maybe it would be best if I returned to the city where

I belong."

Kate realised Alicia was probably facing away from her because she was crying. Thinking back to Laura in the Squirrel Inn, she said, "Hey! I understand not everyone in the countryside shares their view. They are a minority. Just a very vocal one."

"They're also very wealthy and influential," Alicia pointed out, sounding defeated.

"Bullies if you ask me. Why don't you stand up to them and contact the police? They might be able to offer you some type of protection."

Alicia re-joined Kate at the table. "I doubt it. They don't do anything to stop them hunting. The ban is a complete waste of time."

Kate watched Alicia fidgeting and straightening the placemats. She didn't want to upset her again, but Helen's assertions the vandalism wasn't directed at Alicia and Richard worried her. "Going back to Helen. She said something similar to me. About it not being all about you and Richard. What do you think she means? Do you think she could know something about what's behind the attacks?"

"No," Alicia replied, adamantly. "She's just a child. This mess is all my fault. I seem to have upset everyone, including my daughter. I thought she was okay about Richard and me. She said she liked him. Now, they can hardly look at each other."

"The move here must have been a bit of an upheaval. Did she have a lot of friends before you moved?" Kate asked.

"That's why I suggested she spend some time with her old friends. She's the one who chose to come back here." Wringing her hands, Alicia added, "I'm sorry. Do you want more coffee?"

Kate shook her head. "What were you arguing about this morning?"

Alicia slumped lower in her chair. "It was so out of character for her. She knows if she needs something, she only has to ask." She paused to take a deep breath. "I caught her taking my debit card out of my bag."

"Oh. Any idea what she wanted it for?"

"She refused to say. That's what started the argument. She knows the pin number as she's used it before with my permission. I can't think what she would want money for out here. If it was to rent a movie or buy some clothes online, she knows I would agree once I was satisfied that they were suitable. It makes no sense at all. Are you sure I can't get you another coffee?"

"No. I should get going." Pushing herself up and away from the table, Kate asked, "Do you know who owns the sheep along the lane? The ones in the field adjacent to where Richard had his accident?"

Alicia crossed the room and frantically pulled out drawers. "Yes. I have his name and number here, somewhere. A few weeks back, the sheep escaped onto the road. The field is owned by the woman who runs the Wind Whistle. I rang to tell her. She abruptly told me to contact their owner." Retrieving a piece of paper from the last drawer she'd searched, she said, "Here you are. Ben Teobald. He, at least, was polite and thanked me when I rang him on this number to tell him his sheep were wandering up the lane. I'll copy it down for you."

# CHAPTER SEVENTEEN

Simon followed Helen through the rear garden. She disappeared down steep steps to a part of the garden not visible from the house. He negotiated the steps as Helen clambered onto a tyre, swinging from the branches of an old Oak tree.

He returned her angry scowl, with a cheerful, "Hello!"

"What do you want?" Helen asked angrily.

"I wanted to check you were okay. You looked upset."

"I'm absolutely fantastic, can't you see? My life is wonderful!" Helen crumpled forward over the top of the tyre, hiding her face. She raised her head and, with a softer expression, said, "Sorry." She mustered a small smile. "I'm doing as well as can be expected, considering my life has gone to hell in a handcart." Giving a false laugh, she muttered, "Hey! Mustn't grumble."

Simon sat cross-legged on a patch of grass directly in front of the tyre swing. "That bad? Huh?"

Dangling her arms over the rim of the tyre, Helen said, "I know, I'm being a cow. I'll apologise to Mum later." She swung backwards and forwards a few times. She abruptly stopped the swing with her feet. "God! I hate it here. I may as well kill myself."

"Whoa! Nothing is that bad. Why don't you tell me what's wrong?" Lowering his head, trying to catch her attention, he said, "It might help if you talked about it?"

Helen gave a heavy sigh and slumped even further forward. Facing the ground, she said, "It won't help. I've been a complete idiot. No one to blame except me. I don't expect anyone will want to speak to me soon."

"Come on, Helen. What's this about? Do you know something

about the recent attacks?"

"Possibly. Maybe it is all my fault. If I hadn't been so stupid, none of it would be happening."

"You need to explain. Richard could have been killed," Simon said.

Tears welled up in Helen's eyes. "You think I don't know that? Mum is making herself ill with worry. Thinking it's all her fault."

"You need to tell me what's going on."

"I can't. I feel so stupid. I don't want anyone to know. If it all comes out, everyone will hate me. I won't be able to face anyone again. It would be better if I killed myself. Then everything would stop, and I wouldn't have to live with the shame."

"If you tell me, I promise I won't tell another living soul." Simon marked out a cross on his chest with his finger. "I promise. Maybe I could help you sort the problem out."

Helen shook her head. "But then you'd know. I can't."

Simon racked his brain, trying to think of a way to get Helen to open up to him. He couldn't imagine what Helen could have done to set off the chain of events or why she was so fearful of telling anyone what she'd done. Watching her, gently push herself forward and backwards in the tyre, he recognised something he saw every day in Kate. And in himself after the explosion, before he found acting the fool was a better defence mechanism. The mood swings and lashing out at those closest to her. What could Helen have done that was so bad?

Pulling at the grass in front of him, Simon sensed killing herself wasn't an idle threat. She meant it. He looked to the sky and back at Helen. He had to find out what she'd done, however painful the extraction was. "I did something once that destroyed the lives of everyone around me. At night, when I'm alone, the guilt eats away at me. It's not something I ever talk about. Even Kate doesn't know."

Helen lifted her head, her interest piqued. Hesitantly, she asked, "What did you do?"

Continuing to pull handfuls of grass, Simon replied, "If I tell you, will you keep it to yourself?"

Helen nodded her head. "Sure."

"And will you tell me, your secret?"

"You'll hate me."

"You might hate me." Only the sound of the grass being ripped from the earth could be heard. "Do we have a deal?"

After a long silence, Helen quietly replied, "Yes."

"My sister, Rosie, was about your age. Maybe a tad younger. She was crazy about this American singer. For her birthday, I bought us concert tickets to see her. We had a joke about how she would miss the last song. I have a thing about crowds, so I always leave concerts early to avoid the crush. I told her that way I could keep her safe." Simon fell silent, his eyes focused somewhere in the distance as he played with the pile of grass he'd made.

"Go on," Helen urged. "Although I can't see the problem. You sound like a brilliant, big brother. I wish I had one to take me to concerts."

Simon spread out the pile of grass and wrapped his arms around his raised knees. "Only I didn't. A girl I'd fancied for ages rang me a couple of days before the concert, wanting to know if we could meet up for a drink. I cancelled on Rosie. She went to the concert with a friend, Suzie. Suzie's parents took them, and my parents went to pick them up."

As Helen had slowed her swinging, Simon had started to rock gently. "They were waiting in the foyer for the girls to come out. That's when the bomb went off."

"Did they ...?"

"Only Suzie survived. She was badly injured, but she lived."

Helen slipped from the tyre and knelt beside Simon. "I'm so sorry. You can't blame yourself for what happened."

"Oh, but I do. Don't you see? If I had taken Rosie, we would have left before the explosion." Simon angrily rubbed his eyes. "Damn hay fever."

Helen tentatively rubbed Simon's back. "You didn't do anything wrong. Bloody terrorists. They were responsible. Not you."

"Thanks." Simon gave Helen a quick smile. "Sorry, I shouldn't have ...I'm fine, honest."

The angry teenager was gone. In front of Simon was a face full of innocence, compassion and kindness. He shouldn't have burdened her with his baggage. More guilt to add to the tally.

At risk of disappearing into a well of self-pity, Simon remembered why he'd told his story. "Only you know about this. Keep it to yourself, yeah?"

"Promise. Why haven't you told your girlfriend? You seem close?"

"She's not my girlfriend. When I met her, she was in a bad place. Helping her, helped me in a roundabout way. If I had told her then, it would have sounded like I was competing. A one-upmanship on grief. There's never been a suitable time since. Anyway, that's my big screw-up." He softened his voice, "Your turn."

Helen stiffened and shrank back. She changed from kneeling to sitting with her arms wrapped around her drawn-up knees, mirroring Simon's position. Looking at the ground, she said, "I did something stupid. Unlike you, I've brought all this misery on myself. Mum will freak out if she ever finds out. She's always going on about online security and trolls. As for Richard, I'll never be able to stay under the same roof. It will be too embarrassing."

"You're going to have to start at the beginning," Simon said.

"Here is boring. I don't know anyone. The few people of my age I've met are unfriendly. I miss my old home and friends and I have to rely on social media to keep up to date with things. Sometimes, just to have someone to talk to."

"That's understandable. Nothing wrong with that."

"For Mum's sake, I tried to make the most of things. I looked online for local groups. Youth clubs, tennis clubs. Anything I thought would be worth joining. I received a couple of friend requests. I guess they saw my posts saying I was new to the area. There was this guy. Jake. He said he lived here but was at boarding school. We arranged to meet up when he came home for the holidays. We got chatting online. A lot. He totally got me. It was like we'd known each other for years. I was so excited about seeing him. Nervous as hell but looking forward to it."

Helen stopped talking. Simon had a horrible feeling he knew what was coming next. Helen had dropped her head, so her hair was covering her face. Simon could see tears dripping from her chin. He reached forward and squeezed her arm. "It's okay."

Helen pulled her arm away. "It's not okay. Things will never be okay again." Her voice hardened and became bitter. "So, yes, I was a fool. Desperate to have a boyfriend in this godforsaken place, I fell for it, hook, line and sinker. He said he wanted pictures of me ... You know. Sexual ones. Then, videos. He told me he was deleting them straight after. No one else would ever see them. And like the gullible idiot I am, I believed him."

Simon clenched his fists in anger as Helen sobbed. Frustrated she wouldn't let him comfort her in any way, he got to his feet and paced. When the sobs died down, he sat back down next to Helen. This time she didn't pull away when he put his arms around her.

Helen mumbled into Simon's chest, "And now he wants money. If I don't give him £5000, he's going to paste the pictures everywhere. My life will be ruined. How will I ever face anyone again? I'll be a laughingstock at school. Mum will be disappointed beyond words, and Richard will be disgusted. Just the thought of him seeing the pictures is enough. That's what we were arguing about this morning. Mum caught me trying to take her debit card from her purse."

"How has he asked you to send the money?"

"He hasn't said, yet."

Simon put both hands on Helen's shoulders and pulled her around to face him. "Listen. There may be a way out of this. Do you have any idea who this guy is?"

Helen shook her head. "I think his account was fake, and he was using someone else's pictures. If only, I had thought to check him out thoroughly, I might have spotted something."

"Don't dwell on what can't be changed. He's unlikely to want to show his face. My guess is he'll either ask you to leave the cash somewhere or to pay it directly into an account. That's when I'll get him."

Hope shone in Helen's tear-filled eyes. "You could do that?"

"If he wants the cash hidden somewhere, it'll be easy. I'll wait for him to appear. It'll be trickier if he wants a cash transfer. I have a few tricks up my sleeve when it comes to computers. Even better, I have a friend who owes me a favour and who can hack just about anything. So, come on. Dry your eyes. Let me know when he asks for the money, and I can sort this."

"But I haven't got £5000."

"Don't worry about that. I have. Remind me again how old you are?"

"Nearly fifteen."

Simon pulled Helen to her feet. "Dry your eyes and stop worrying. I've got this."

Helen wiped her face dry and smiled. "You'd do this for me?" Worry returned to her face. "You won't have to tell anyone else or see the pictures, will you?"

"No one other than me needs to know the full details," Simon said. "Now, go and make it up with your mum."

Helen gave him a quick kiss on the cheek. She blushed afterwards. "Thank you. Thank you. Thank you." She went to leave, then hesitated. "I am so sorry about your family. What happened was awful, but not your fault."

Simon cringed. One of the many reasons he didn't tell people was the platitudes. He knew people were trying to help, to be kind, but he found the pointlessness of the words and their inadequacy grated. He gave his usual response of a shrug, and a mumbled, "Thanks." He felt sick to his stomach. Ashamed not only that he'd used the horrific event to manipulate, but also to have dumped something so huge on a vulnerable, young girl. The fact she was so thankful, and her face expressed something close to hero-worship made it worse. He hoped to God, he would be able to unearth the creep who'd tricked her so cruelly. He felt Helen was waiting for something more. What, he had no idea. He had already cowardly played his trump card.

Helen made a circle in the ground with her toe. "The things

that have been going on here. The horse, the gate and the car. Do you think it is related to the images?"

The same thought had gone through Simon's mind earlier. It was possible, but something about it didn't fit right. He didn't want to upset Helen by saying, if there was a connection, it would probably be the other way around. If someone was hell-bent on punishing Richard and Alicia any way they could, this might be the chosen route to torturing their daughter. He gave what he hoped was a reassuring smile. "My gut feeling is no. If I find out differently when I catch the sick creep, then I'll deal with it. Stop worrying. All you have to do is come and find me the next time he contacts you."

# CHAPTER EIGHTEEN

Simon met Kate leaving the cottage carrying her riding hat. "Where are you off to?"

"Alicia said I could ride Paddy."

"Go careful."

"I will. I'm not planning on leaving the grounds. I'm going to school him in the paddock."

"Did you find out anything more?" Nodding in the direction of the main house, Simon asked, "Have they contacted the police?"

"Not yet. I only spoke to Alicia. Richard was still asleep. I can't work out why she's so against contacting them. I'm hoping Richard will talk some sense into her. I would feel safer tonight if I thought someone was looking into things."

"What do you think I'm doing?"

"Oh. There was something else. The field adjacent to where Richard fell is owned by the landlady of the Wind Whistle. And guess who she rents it to for their sheep?"

"Enlighten me."

"Ben Teobald. You remember. The blond guy who bought us a drink."

"Interesting. Let's hope he's in there when we pay a visit tonight. Otherwise, I'll track him down tomorrow."

"Did you find out what's bothering Helen? Her mother caught her trying to steal money this morning," Kate said. "She's worried about her."

"I did, but I can't tell you anything more as I made a promise. You go and enjoy your ride. I've got a couple of phone calls to make."

Early evening, Kate and Simon set off for the Wind Whistle Inn in Alicia's Mini. Kate had refused to eat there, convinced the chef would probably spit on their food, so they'd compromised on a few drinks before going to another pub Alicia had recommended for food. Alicia had insisted they take her Mini rather than manoeuvre the camper van through the narrow lanes. She hadn't done anything about repairing the windscreen on the Range Rover, but Richard also had a car. Simon and Kate could hang onto the Mini until they left, and Alicia would drive Richard's Porsche. Alicia admitted Richard hated getting in and out of her Mini and continuously moaned about the lack of legroom, so in all probability, she would end up ferrying him around in the Porsche, whether they took the Mini or not.

The same frosty atmosphere as on their previous visit met them inside the pub. The dark interior and foreboding silence brought Kate out in goosebumps. Simon put a protective arm around her shoulder as she tensed and fidgeted with the car keys. The woman behind the bar, who they assumed was the landlady, continued to talk to a group of locals, keeping them waiting to be served. They both watched their drinks being poured in case of any spitting.

Turning from the bar to find somewhere to sit, their way was blocked by Ben.

"Hi, again. Good to see you back in here. I was worried Jade had frightened you away."

"Here's the nearest place for a drink, and we don't scare that easy," Simon replied pleasantly, meeting Ben's smile with one of his own. "There is something I'd like to ask you about."

"Fire away," Ben replied, seemingly unconcerned by anything they might ask.

"Shall we go outside?" Simon said, nodding towards the entrance. "It's another lovely evening."

"Anvil!" A gruff voice shouted across the bar. "Where are you going? It's your round." A group of people huddled around a table viewed them suspiciously. Two raised empty pint glasses into the air. "We're dying of thirst over here."

Ben shouted back, "They're on their way." He said to Simon, "I'll see you outside in five minutes."

Kate and Simon didn't wait long before Ben joined them with a fresh pint. He seated himself on the opposite side of their table and raised his glass. "Cheers." He drank deeply, about a third of the glass emptying in one gulp. He wiped his mouth with the back of his hand. "I needed that. Been a long, hard day."

"Why did they call you Anvil? I thought your name was Ben?" Kate asked.

"It is. Anvil is a nickname. I'm a farrier."

"So, you'd be comfortable around horses of all types," Simon said.

"I suppose I would be."

"Even difficult ones. Ones that were difficult to shoe."

"I guess," Ben replied, looking perplexed.

"Do you have any that need sedation?" Simon asked.

"A few could probably do with some," Ben joked. "Only the owners think their behaviour is endearing. I don't think they appreciate how hard it is to do a good job when their little darling is swinging its legs about." He took a drink and screwed up his face in thought. "I think there's two that the owners give Sedalin to before I arrive. Not that I'm convinced it does much to calm them."

"Do you carry any horse calmers with you?" Simon asked.

Ben laughed. "I wish." Chuckling into his pint, he admitted, "I'd probably end up giving it to the owners instead. Half the time, they're the problem anyway. Not the horse. Why do you ask?"

"Just interested."

"What was it you wanted to ask me?" Ben asked.

"The sheep next to the lane leading from Clenchers Mill. We understand they're yours?" Kate said.

"I part share them with my little brother. He does all the looking after. I pop out there now and again to check them over.

And the fencing. Right little Houdini's, some of them. Have they been getting out again?"

"We've not seen any of them out. Would you have been checking them on the day of Richard's accident? Friday at about three o'clock?" Simon asked.

Ben rubbed his chin, his forehead creased as he thought. He pulled out his phone and flicked through a few apps. "I keep my diary on here." Reading from the screen, he said, "Friday at three o'clock, I was shoeing over at the Pearce's. Their place is about ten miles away in the opposite direction. So, definitely not on Friday around that time." Flicking through screens, he added, "The Thursday before was the last time I was over there. The time before that was when Alicia rang me to say they were out on the road. Harry promised he'd put a new battery on the fencer. I went to check that he had."

"Does anyone exercise their dogs in that field?" Kate asked.

"Hopefully, not. There's no footpath through there. Most around here know to stay out of fields with livestock." After a pause, he added, "You might want to check with Sue Evans. She means well. She gets all hot and bothered when the sheep get tangled up in the brambles. I've told her repeatedly that they generally free themselves when they want to, but she will keep checking and calling me if she sees one caught up. Harry visits them every morning and evening, so he would spot any that got into real difficulty."

"Would your brother be happy to talk to us about whether he was in the field on Friday?" Simon asked.

Ben's smile faltered, and he lifted his glass to his lips to avoid the question. Placing it back on the table, he asked, "Are you enjoying your stay?"

"Wonderful," Simon replied. "Your brother. How can we contact him?"

Ben stood up. "He's inside with Jade. She's underage, but at least I can keep an eye on them, here. Friday at three o'clock, you said. I'll go and ask him."

"I'd prefer to ask him myself. How old is your brother?" Simon asked.

"Eighteen."

"An adult, then. Able to speak for himself," Simon said.

Ben's forehead creased, and he drank from his pint. Placing the empty glass on the table, he said, "I'll have a word with him."

"Why don't you want us to speak to him?" Kate asked.

"He's with the others, and it will be easier if I ask him," Ben said. "Look, I don't want any trouble. My brother might put on an act to impress Jade and the others. He's had problems in the past, but he's starting to get his act together, and I want to keep it that way. That's why I bought the sheep. He's good with animals. It's people and life generally he has a problem with."

"What's your view on blood sports?" Kate asked, as he turned to leave.

"Around here, it's a way of life, and it's my livelihood. A fair chunk of the horses I shoe are hunters."

"Do you follow the hunt?" Simon asked.

"I occasionally go out on the back of a quad bike with the terrier boys, but the day itself is more of a social thing for me. I generally meet them back in the pub, afterwards."

"That doesn't answer the question," Simon said. "What do you really think? Do you shoot?"

Ben sighed and retook his seat at the table. "I have been out on pheasant shoots. Again, more of a social event for me. I think people who don't understand how the countryside works shouldn't try to interfere. It's a bit like the Woodstock song. You know? They paved paradise and put up a parking lot."

"How do you mean?" Kate asked.

"Field sports are a way of life devised to protect the countryside. Farmers love and understand their land. They wouldn't do it otherwise," Ben said, leaning forward. "But they get hit from all sides. People demand cheap food without appreciating what it costs to produce. Farmers do the job for love, but they need to make a living and protect their livestock and crops. It's the cheap prices demanded that impact animals' welfare. With arable farming, it leads to more chemicals to increase yields. Farmers know the true cost to the land. Many won't do it. They'd prefer to sell up the land that has been farmed by their family for generations. Many commit suicide. Did you know more than one farmer a week commits suicide in this country?"

"No, I didn't," Kate replied, visibly shocked.

"Their land gets sucked up into bigger and bigger farms. Owned by corporations with their eyes purely on profit. The animals that once had names and grazed the fields are given a number and spend their lives indoors in tiny pens. That's animal cruelty and far worse than hunting."

"You're straying from the point," Simon interrupted. "You know as well as I do, hunting is all about the day's *sport*, not controlling numbers."

"I agree with Ben about farming. I avoid factory-farmed meat wherever possible," Kate said.

"Soon, that will be the only option," Ben said.

"I'd become a vegetarian at that point," Kate replied.

"And fields will be turned into ugly rows of greenhouses to feed the demand." Colour rose in Ben's cheeks as he continued, earnestly, "People, like your friends up at Clenchers Mill who move to the countryside because of its beauty. They won't be so impressed with the view. As the farms are sold, the farmhouses aren't needed. They're turned into fancy retreats and spas. Londoners move here for the country air, pushing up house prices, so the youngsters who would have worked on the land are priced out. Proper established communities are being replaced by commuters who give nothing back to the area. Turning what initially appealed to them into the suburban hell, they thought they wanted to escape."

"Are you saying people not lucky enough to be brought up in the countryside, can't live here? That the countryside should be purely for countryfolk?" Simon said.

"No. I'm simply saying that if they choose to move to the countryside, they should try to fit in and respect the local traditions. Not seek to change and destroy a way of life because they don't understand it."

"Is that what you think Alicia and Richard are doing?" Simon asked.

"That's exactly what they're doing. And then crying foul when people retaliate," Ben said, forcefully.

"By drugging their horse and throwing a dead fox through their car windscreen?" Simon fired back.

Startled, Ben exclaimed, "What? No! When did that happen?"

"You're saying you know nothing about the intimidation they've suffered?" Simon persisted.

"I'm aware people haven't gone out of their way to be friendly and welcoming because of their plans for the Clencher Mill. I've not heard anything along the lines you're suggesting. That's dreadful."

"Their horse narrowly missed being put to sleep. It had been given hallucinogenic drugs," Kate said.

Ben's eyes widened. "The one Richard fell off? I thought the horse just spooked at something, and he couldn't control it."

Kate nodded her head. "You don't know anything about it? Not heard rumours or gossip about who was behind it?"

"No way! I don't know anyone who would do something like that." Protectively, he added, "Neither does my brother."

"You sure?" Simon asked.

"Nobody around here would do something like that! It's the antis who use violence and intimidation. Not us." Ben stood up from the table. "Is this why you want to speak to my brother? Are you going to accuse him of doing something to that horse? Harry loves animals and would never do something so cruel."

"We're not accusing either of you of anything. We want to know if he was in the field at the time of the accident and whether he saw anything," Kate said, trying to calm the situation."

Ben turned abruptly toward the pub entrance. "I'll see if he wants to speak to you."

# CHAPTER NINETEEN

While they were waiting, Kate rang Mark Oates. Ending the call, she shook her head. "He's adamant it was a man he saw in the field, so I don't think it could have been Sue Evans."

Harry and Jade sauntered out of the pub, ten minutes later. Jade carried their two drinks while Harry tapped away at his phone screen, studying it intently. He had his brother's facial features but was shorter and skinny.

Jade walked to the adjacent table and put down the glasses. She sat on the table with her feet on a chair, staring at Kate aggressively.

Harry came to a halt in front of their table. Without looking up from his phone, he drawled, "Anvil said you wanted to ask me something about my sheep."

"How often do you check on them, and do you go at any particular time of the day?" Simon asked.

"What's it to you?" Harry replied defensively, his fingers and thumbs typing furiously on this phone.

Jade stood up on the chair. "Don't tell them, Harry. They're bloody vegans, I bet. They probably want to sneak in and steal the fluffy, wuffy things when they know you're not about." Sitting down on the table, she directed her attitude at Kate. "Are you one of those vegans? I bet you don't shave your armpits either." She pinched her nose between her forefinger and thumb. "Phewy. There's a sour stink around here."

Simon threw Jade a dismissive look and turned his attention back to Harry. "I'd like to know if you would have been in the field around three o'clock, last Friday. The afternoon Richard fell from his horse?"

Still preoccupied with his phone, Harry said, "Nah. Shame. I'd have liked to see him come a cropper. And the air ambulance. I've not seen one up close. I heard it go over, mind."

"I reckon they're well fit, those air ambulance men. Wish I'd been there and all," Jade said.

Ignoring Jade, Simon asked Harry, "Where were you when the ambulance came in to land?"

"I was in here. You can check if you like. A group of us came out to take a gander when we heard it flying over. Wondering who it was and all. I think someone said it might have been to do with Clenchers. Considering where it came down, like."

Becoming irritated by Harry's obsession with his phone, Simon said, "Any chance you could put that away while we're talking? Can you remember who said the ambulance would be for someone from Clenchers Mill?"

Raising his phone slightly, Harry replied, "Nah." Indicating the phone screen, he added, "This is well important. What did you say again?"

Giving an irritated snort, Simon said, "Who suggested the air ambulance was for someone at Clenchers Mill?"

Looking up briefly to sneer, Harry replied, "Can't remember. Tasty daughter, mind."

"Oi!" Jade said.

"She's got a cute little mole." Harry tore himself away from his phone screen long enough to point to his left upper chest. "About here."

Simon leapt forward. His larger frame dwarfed Harry's. He grabbed the front of Harry's shirt in his right hand and snatched the phone with his left hand.

Harry squealed, "Hey! Give that back."

Jade bounced up and down on the table. "Yeah, that's theft. Give it back."

Holding the squirming Harry at arm's length, Simon exited from the cricket results Harry had been checking and opened the photo album. He scrolled through the pictures with his left thumb. His eyes widened in shock and narrowed in anger when he got to one batch. He glared at Harry, who gave him a sly grin. Simon shook his head in despair and continued to scroll. His forehead furrowed as he squinted at the screen.

"Like mother, like daughter, eh?" Harry mocked with a smug grin.

"Getting an eyeful?" Jade taunted, "Liking it, are you? Don't suppose your frigid, vegan girlfriend does it for you. I could always help you out."

"Shut up," Simon growled, as he continued to scroll. He'd had a pre-warning about Helen's pictures, but the photographs of Alicia when she was younger, working as a lap dancer, took him by surprise. The next set of photographs and videos made him sick to the stomach. A tubby boy wearing round glasses that magnified his eyes, sat naked as he masturbated. Incandescent with anger and disgust, Simon looked up at Harry.

The smug grin fell from Harry's face when he realised what he and Jade found hilarious, wasn't being viewed in the same way.

"You sick, vile, cruel creature!" Simon snarled. Turning the phone screen to face him, he asked, "Is this the boy who committed suicide? The boy, that people claim killed himself because he was being bullied for his hunting activities?"

"Err. I'm not sure." Harry reached for his phone. "Give it back so I can see."

Simon held the phone out of his reach. "You don't know what indecent images are on your phone?" he said, slipping the phone into his back pocket.

"Hey! Give that back!" Harry shouted, struggling to release himself from Simon's grip. He clawed at Simon's fist.

In response, Simon tightened his hold on the front of his shirt.

"Stop. You're strangling me."

Jade slid from the table. "I'll go get Anvil and the guys." Looking up at Simon, she added, "They'll sort you out good and proper." She hesitated, listening to what Simon said to Harry.

"You sure you want your friends out here? How do you think they're going to react to the news that you drove that young boy to suicide?" Simon tightened his grip on Harry's shirt again and raised his fist, forcing him onto his tiptoes. He felt he could happily throttle the boy and his loudmouth girlfriend. "He was well-liked within the hunting community, wasn't he? I've seen the collection box for his family at the bar. His dad looks a burly sort. I wonder how he will react when he knows why his son killed himself?"

"He was being bullied at school. He told me all about it. I've got names," Jade protested.

Never taking his eyes off Harry, Simon said, "Was it you or Jade posing online as his girlfriend?"

"We were never going to share the pictures," Harry said.

"You just threatened to, so he would give you money."

"We were just messing about," Harry protested.

Simon twisted Harry's shirt front. "You thought it was funny, did you? You do realise you could go to prison for this, don't you? Not just for extortion. Having pornographic images of minors is an offence. You'll be put on the sexual offenders' list. For life. Any idea what happens in prison to paedophiles?"

Harry trembled and looked like he might cry. "I'm not one of them."

Less sure of herself, Jade said without any conviction, "They're faking it. Shall I get the others?"

Keeping his attention on Harry's terrified eyes, Simon turned his head slightly and said, "It's worse what they do in women's prisons." Turning his head back to Harry, he asked, "Who else has seen these?"

"Just us two."

Turning to face Jade, Simon said, "Give your phone to Kate."

"No, I won't," Jade protested. "You can't make me."

"Do it, Jade," Harry said. "I think they can."

Kate, who had watched events unfold in stunned silence, took a gulp of her drink and held out her hand for the phone. With a great deal of huffing and puffing, Jade pulled out her phone and slammed it into Kate's open palm.

"Are the images stored anywhere else? On laptops, maybe?"

Simon asked.

"No," Harry replied.

"Here's what we're going to do," Simon said, releasing his hold on Harry. "You see, I don't believe you. We're going to follow you to your homes. There, you're going to show me what other devices you have and all the images you have saved. Any I don't like the look of, you're going to delete in front of me. Okay?"

"Will you do the same with the phones?" Harry asked.

"I might. Or I might keep them as a form of insurance. You never know when I might hand them in to the police, saying I found them. They'll be very interested in the images, I'm sure."

"You can't do that? My whole life is on my phone," Jade shrieked.

"Maybe it's time you got a new life," Simon replied. "Come on. We're going to follow you home in our car."

Ben appeared in the pub doorway, holding a fresh pint of beer. "Everything okay, out here?"

Giving Harry a quick warning look, Simon replied, "We're good."

Ben gave his brother a quizzical look. "You sure?"

"Yeah, bro," Harry replied. "I'm giving Jade a lift home. She's not feeling too good."

"Okay. I'll see you at home later," Ben said, before disappearing back inside.

# CHAPTER TWENTY

Harry and Jade sat in sullen silence after all the images and copy correspondence they'd shared to their laptops had been deleted. Simon left them dangling, by saying he would decide over the next couple of days what to do about their phones, which remained safely stored in his pocket.

When Simon and Kate emerged from the house Jade shared with her parents, the sun was sinking into a bank of clouds hovering over the horizon. Neither of them had eaten, and they quickly decided to drive back to the pub they'd passed earlier before they stopped serving food.

Waiting for their food to arrive in the Little Wool Pit Inn, Kate said, "I was wrong about you. You are a dark horse. I was worried back there you were going to kill those two. I've never seen you so angry and aggressive. Not that they didn't deserve it."

"Harry and Jade got right under my skin. I've never wanted to seriously hurt anyone before. But those two. I still feel so agitated by what they did."

"What do you plan on doing with the phones? Are you going to hand them in to the police?" Kate asked.

"I've not decided yet. I promised Helen that no one else would ever find out about what she did. Please, don't let on to her that you know anything."

"Okay. What about the rest of it?" Kate asked. "From the little you've told me, Helen's pictures didn't come as a surprise, but Alicia's did. And there's that poor boy who killed himself because of the games they were playing."

"I'm guessing those images are why Alicia has been so anxious. It also explains her reluctance to report anything to the police.

She probably lied or forgot to mention that part of her life to Richard and is worried about how he'll react."

"You've known him for longer. Would he end their relationship over it?"

"I don't know him well enough to say," Simon replied, after giving the matter some thought.

"If he did, that suggests the relationship was shallow, anyway. Her bank balance would take a hit, but in the long term, she'd be better off without him," Kate said.

"Either way, the decision will be hers. I'll speak to her tomorrow after I've spoken to Helen. It'll be their call whether I delete their images or take them to the police," Simon said.

"And the boy? The one they drove to suicide?"

Simon intertwined his fingers behind his head and leaned back. "I honestly don't know what to do for the best. If I go to the police, Harry and Jade will be punished, but what will it be like for the boy's parents? They're still reeling from his death. Would the possibility of those images leaking out cause them more upset?"

"At least they'd know why he killed himself. They'd have a reason to hold onto instead of blaming themselves for failing their son in some way," Kate said.

"Do you think? Or will it make things worse? They'll still think they should have noticed how upset he was in the weeks leading up to his death. They'll just have the added burden of those images."

"You could be right," Kate accepted, leaning back in her chair. "Did you believe them when they said drugging the horse and the other vandalism had nothing to do with them?"

"Not entirely. Time will tell on that one," Simon said. "It's the type of thing they would find funny."

Kate was about to say something more when their food arrived. A rump steak for Simon and pork belly with apricot stuffing for Kate. Their meals were excellent and eaten in appreciative silence.

Kate finished first. She sat back from the table, rubbing her bloated stomach. "That was delicious, but I'm not going to manage a dessert."

Simon looked at his plate and blew out his cheeks. "This has almost got me beat, but I'm determined to finish."

Kate watched Simon resume eating. "I missed out on a run this morning. I'll have to run double tomorrow to work this off." Receiving only a nod from Simon, she continued, "Other than the fact I was shattered from not having any sleep, I didn't feel safe enough to leave the grounds early in the morning by myself."

Simon stopped chewing. "But you'll feel safe enough to go for a run tomorrow?"

"You said yourself, the gate prank was probably the work of those two. The same possibly goes for the unpleasant gift of the dead fox through the windscreen."

"What about drugging the horse? Ben was adamant his brother loved animals."

"Harry didn't seem that bright," Kate said. "He might not have appreciated how violently the horse would react."

"I guess."

"We've uncovered the blackmail threats Alicia and Helen have been receiving, and if it was Harry and Jade, then the attacks will stop, so we can think about leaving."

"Maybe, but we don't know for sure it was Harry and Jade," Simon pointed out. "And what do I tell Richard?"

"Tricky, if Alicia doesn't want to admit to the blackmail. If you're not going to hand the phones to the police, I don't see what else we can do here."

"Do you really think Ben had no idea what his brother was doing?" Simon asked.

"My gut feeling is no."

"Can I give my final decision on what to do after I've spoken to everyone tomorrow?"

"You'll have to go over early," Kate replied. "Alicia is taking Richard for a hospital appointment in the morning?"

"Oh, yes. I'd forgotten. Can you knock on my door first thing in the morning? And make sure I'm getting up?"

"No problem, but I can't imagine they'll be leaving that early. How about I make sure you're up when I get back from my run?" Kate replied, trying to get comfortable.

Simon nodded. "That'll work."

Rubbing her side, Kate said, "I've eaten so much, I'm not sure I can move."

"You probably need fattening up, anyway." Pushing his plate into the centre of the table, Simon said, "I'm done. Do you want another drink before we go?"

"I don't think I have room even for another drink." Playing with her half-full glass, Kate asked, "Have you ever done it?"

Simon pulled a confused face. "Umm, you'll have to clarify what you mean. I've done a lot of things."

"You know. Sextexting, or whatever it is they call it."

Simon shook his head. "Can't say as I have. You?"

"Nope. I've never even considered it. I don't see the attraction."

"Me neither, but teenagers live their lives online. I guess if you're a fourteen-year-old, with raging hormones and no friends nearby, it's a bit different." Chuckling, Simon added, "I'm pleased there's no digital record of the things I got up to at that age. Social media wasn't so invasive when I was young, and I wasn't foolish enough to leave a trail."

"My parents wouldn't even let me have a Facebook account until I was sixteen," Kate said, with a pained expression. "Now children seem to have an account as soon as they're able to press a button. Were you surprised at how different their backgrounds were?"

"I guessed from talking to Ben that their family was affluent. I thought Jade's family were probably not as wealthy, but I was surprised at how run down the house was." Stretching his arms up and arching his back, Simon said, "You good to go? I need to force myself to move, or I'm going to seize up."

Kate stood, laughing. "Come on, old man. Time to get you home."

# CHAPTER TWENTY-ONE

Kate's nightmares were less intrusive than the night before, and she returned from her run in a buoyant mood. Her, 'if only' tattoo hadn't been as insistent as usual, and she's spent most of her run mulling over the events of the previous evening. She'd been shocked by Simon's anger, but she'd also been impressed with the way he'd handled things. His loyalty, thoughtfulness and consideration of other people's feelings was a side of Simon she'd not seen before.

He infuriated her at times, but she realised how lucky she'd been to have seen his note that day at the solicitor's. Maybe it was fate. When she moved on, she hoped they'd always remain friends. Her mood was also improved by the thought they'd be leaving soon. The cottage was beautiful, but she hadn't stopped feeling on edge since the morning she'd found the dead crows.

She knocked on Simon's door, shouting, "Get up, sleepyhead," on her way to the shower. She waited outside his door until she heard groans and sounds of movement and continued along the hallway. She shouted out, "Good job, I didn't wake you before my run," before closing the bathroom door behind her.

Refreshed, she entered the kitchen. Simon was already there with a pot of coffee made and toast cooling on the rack. She gratefully poured herself a coffee and buttered a piece of toast. Leaning against the counter, she asked, "What's the plan?"

Simon glanced at his watch. "If we get over there quick, I'm hoping to catch Alicia by herself. I get the feeling Richard isn't a morning person."

Kate pushed herself off the counter and buttered a second piece of toast. She took a slurp of coffee and said, "I'm good to go. I can eat the toast on the way over."

Walking out the door, Simon said, "After Alicia, I'd like to talk to Helen. Alone."

They found Alicia nervously pacing her kitchen. Despite her smiles and nervous energy, she looked drained and exhausted, with dark rings under her eyes. She seemed lost in her stylish fawn trousers and white shirt. Kate couldn't imagine Alicia making a mistake over her dress size, so she assumed she'd lost weight through all her worrying. Alicia fussed around them, flitting about the room, offering them drinks and breakfast until Simon persuaded her to sit at the table.

"When are you expecting Richard to come down?"

"We don't need to leave for the hospital for another forty minutes," Alicia replied, her eyes darting to the wall clock. "He'll probably breeze in two minutes before we're due to leave and then urge me to drive faster all the way there. He knows I don't like to drive fast. Porsche or no Porsche." Despite her words, she persistently checked the doorway. She jumped up from her seat and walked towards the door. "Should I call him? He's probably awake."

Simon shook his head. "Come and sit back down. We have some good news, we wanted to share just with you."

Alicia opened her fridge and poured herself an orange juice. "Are you sure you don't want anything?"

"We're fine," Kate replied, indicating Alicia should return to the table.

Hesitantly, Alicia crossed the room and sat in the chair furthest away from them. Her hand trembled when she raised the glass to her lips."

"We think we know why you've been so reluctant to involve the police about Richard's accident and the vandalism," Simon said.

Alicia's eyes widened in surprise, while her hand froze, holding the glass to her lips.

"We've discovered who has been blackmailing you about your

past." Simon pulled Harry's phone from his pocket and placed it on the table. "We also have his phone."

With the glass still frozen in place, Alicia stared at the phone as if it might come to life and attack her.

Simon continued, "I could delete all the images and the messages he sent to you." He left a gap before adding, "Or, I could hold onto it, while you consider whether you want to tell Richard about your past. The phone could then be passed to the police. It's your call."

Alicia slowly lowered the glass, her eyes glued to the blank phone screen. "Everything is on there? And you spoke to the person responsible? You know who has been hounding me?"

"The text messages, yes. They deny causing any damage or doing anything else. We're not convinced one way or the other. They are pro-hunt, but if you contact the police about the intimidation and property damage, they aren't going to retaliate by carrying out their threat to expose you."

Kate added, "If you tell Richard the truth, there would be nothing for them to expose. You could decide whether they should be punished for trying to blackmail you and making your last few weeks, or however long this has been going on for, a living hell."

"Have you seen the pictures and what they were insinuating?" Alicia asked.

Kate shook her head while Simon said, "I only flicked through them."

Alicia was about to say something when they heard heavy footfalls descending the staircase. "That sounds like Richard now." She quickly moved to the other side of the room, near the window. She clapped her hands together, "Why don't you come around for a meal tonight? About eight o'clock? That will give me time to whip up something tasty."

"Yup, that sounds perfect," Simon said. "Kate?"

Seeing a look of relieved gratitude replacing the anxiety on Alicia's face, Kate felt she had no option other than to accept the invitation.

Simon stood and pushed his chair under the table.

Richard hobbled in and said, "Ah! The two detectives," by way of greeting. "Any news for us?"

"We're still working on it," Simon replied.

"I've invited them around for supper. We can talk about it, then," Alicia said, brightly.

As Richard gingerly sat, Kate stood. "I hope your hospital appointment goes well."

Holding the back of the chair, Simon asked Alicia, "Do you know where Helen is?"

Richard rolled his eyes and said, "In her bedroom, playing her music too loud. That's what drove me down here."

"Do you mind if I pop up to have a word with her before we go?" Simon asked.

While Alicia gave him directions to her room, Richard said, "Tell her to turn that blasted music down."

Kate returned to the cottage, while Simon headed upstairs.

# CHAPTER TWENTY-TWO

Not looking forward to the planned evening meal, Kate banged around the cottage, cleaning. She doubted Alicia would tell Richard the truth, so tonight's conversation could become awkward as they'd be forced to skirt around the issue. Surfaces were aggressively wiped until they shone, cushions were thumped until they stood to attention, and the floor gave up all its dirty secrets to her frantic mopping. Still, Simon hadn't reappeared following his talk with Helen. She dumped the mop and bucket back into the cupboard, annoyed he was now trying to avoid her.

Too wired to relax with a book or watch the television, she decided to take Alicia up on her offer of riding Paddy whenever she felt like it. She had discovered that not only was Paddy a perfect gentleman, but unlike Simon, he had been correctly schooled to a good standard. She was so intent on perfecting flying canter changes she hadn't noticed Simon leaning on the post-and-rail fence, watching her. She brought Paddy back to a walk and headed over to him. As she often found, an hour's riding had dispelled her bad mood.

Simon shielded his eyes from the sun as she approached. "Looking good, what I saw of it."

"Thank you," Kate replied, having to work hard to keep from smiling and remember how cross she was with him. "I can see why Cynthia was so adamant he wouldn't go crazy and throw his rider." Leaning forward to pat Paddy's muscular neck, she said, "He's an absolute dream to ride. I'm so pleased Alicia didn't put him down. It would have been unfair and such a waste." Talking to the horse, she added, "You must have been terrified. Who in their right mind would send a horse off on a psychedelic high?"

Simon rested his foot on the bottom rung of the fence. "Who, indeed. I'd love to find out for sure, but if you're adamant about leaving, I'll come with you."

Kate narrowed her eyes. She hated the claustrophobic, sinister atmosphere in the Wind Whistle Inn and was keen to leave, but she didn't think she'd made it a condition they leave immediately.

Simon continued, without giving Kate the chance to say anything, "We've done as Cynthia asked, saved a horse and discovered who was blackmailing Alicia and Helen. I guess that's not too bad a result for my first case."

"What did Helen say?"

"Not much. She's grateful, but also still feels embarrassed by the whole thing. She was mortified by the fact I've seen some of the images." Simon shrugged. "I think me leaving would spare her more blushes."

"Did you tell her who it was?"

"No. I insinuated that it was someone living several miles away rather than virtually on her doorstep. I did insist she contact me straight away if there's even the slightest hint of more trouble. I wouldn't mind seeing Harry and Jade again before we leave to stress I still have their phones and how much trouble they could be in."

"You're not handing the phones over to the police, then?"

"I hope they've learnt their lesson. Unpleasant, though they are, I don't want to ruin their lives. Who knows, maybe I've done them some good, and they'll turn out okay."

"You, big softy," Kate teased. "Walk me back to the paddock. I'll turn Paddy straight out, and you can carry the saddle back to the stables for me."

Simon opened the gate, and they walked towards the paddock. Helen came flying down the driveway to meet them. They could see at once that something was desperately wrong.

Helen skidded to a halt in front of them, and between breathless gasps, with wild eyes and tears streaming down her face, she spluttered, "The police ... telephoned the house ... There's been an accident ... The brakes on the Porsche failed ... They think they were tampered with."

Simon wrapped his arms around Helen, and she sobbed into his chest as Kate helplessly looked on. Helen continued jabbering away between sobs, but her words became too muffled and disjointed to make any sense.

Kate said, "Take Helen back to the cottage. I'll join you as soon as I've sorted Paddy out."

Kate rushed to the cottage to find Helen sitting on the sofa in the living room with her knees pulled up to her chin and her hands wrapped around her legs. With red-rimmed eyes, Helen looked up briefly and nodded a hello. Kate gave her a gentle squeeze on the shoulder as she went to the kitchen, where she could hear Simon's voice. She pulled up a chair to wait for him to finish his telephone conversation.

"That was the hospital," Simon said, ending the call. "They weren't travelling at any great speed. Their injuries are unpleasant, but it could have been a lot more serious."

Unnoticed, Helen had slipped into the kitchen. "Mum always drives slowly. It drives Richard nuts. He drives like a lunatic."

Kate pulled out a chair next to her. "Come and sit down. Can I get you something to eat or drink?"

Helen slid onto the chair but declined any food. Looking up at Simon, she asked, "How are they? Can I visit them?"

"Richard has a broken leg to go with his ribs and arm. Your mum is badly battered and bruised. The hospital wants them to stay in overnight as they both banged their heads in the collision."

"Collision? Was another vehicle involved?" Kate asked.

"No, a tree. When Alicia realised, she had no brakes, she drove into the tree on purpose instead of allowing the car to accelerate down the hill." Turning to Helen, Simon said, "Visiting times don't start for another few hours. Why don't you go next door to pack a few things they might need overnight? I'll rustle up something for us to eat, and then we'll head over there."

Once Helen had left, Kate joined Simon at the counter. "Have you spoken to the police?"

Simon handed Kate a bag of dried pasta. "That's as far as I got," he said, indicating the open cupboard door. "I'll go outside to ring them."

Placing the pasta on the kitchen table behind her, Kate asked, "How much are you going to tell them?"

"I'll tell them about the drugged horse, the crows, the gate and the dead fox thrown through the windscreen. Anything else is up to them." Simon went quiet before saying, "And about the man, Mark Oates saw walking away from an accident scene across the field...And our conversation with Ben."

"You think that's relevant?"

"Um, yeah. I'm going to stress they should speak to Ben," Simon said. "Ben admitted he's fighting to maintain his livelihood and lifestyle, and that Richard and Alicia represent the enemy. He even mentioned the planned retreat. We don't know for sure he doesn't know about the blackmail. Ben also matches the description Mark gave."

"That was so vague it could have been anyone."

"Anyone male with a stocky build who just happens to own the sheep in that field."

"Except he said he was shoeing a horse several miles away," Kate reminded him.

"We've only got his word for it. He gave the name of the people he claimed he was with, didn't he? Pearce, I think he said. See if you can find someone of that name locally and ring them to check."

"Are you going to mention anything at all about the blackmail attempts?"

Simon gave her a frustrated look. "I've given my word to Alicia and Helen on that score. It's not up to me."

"And the boy who killed himself?" Kate asked.

"I'm still thinking about that. I can't see how it is connected to the problems experienced here."

"You saw how aggressive Jade was. If anyone knows anything about the attacks on the family, it'll be those two. And …"

"Yes, family. Ben and his younger brother."

"Shut up, a minute, I'm thinking." Kate paced across the room. Holding her hands out for Simon to stay quiet, she said, "Bear with me here. I'm thinking out loud. The night Alicia's windscreen was smashed, and the alarm woke us … Assuming that was the same night the brakes were tampered with … The damage to Alicia's car may have been merely a distraction." Stopping in front of Simon, she concluded, "The true purpose of the visit was to meddle with the Porsche's brakes."

"Possibly. I admit I didn't check whether the intruder had touched the Porsche," Simon said.

Pacing across the room, Kate said, "What if the property damage and the local resentment to the planned retreat are being used to camouflage something else?"

"You've lost me."

"Drugging the horse and tampering with the Porsche are attacks specifically against Richard. Someone wanting him, at best, seriously injured. You heard what Helen said. Richard likes driving at speed. If he had been driving, the accident could have been very different. Glueing gates and leaving dead animals is unpleasant, but it's not life-threatening."

"Okay. My head is hurting following the logic and the implications, but I see the point you're making," Simon said. "Let me speak to the police. I'm still going to suggest they start their enquiries with Ben Teobald. You see if you can speak to the Pearce family, and we'll see where we go from there."

# CHAPTER TWENTY-THREE

After ending the call to Penny Pearce, Kate stared at the receiver while deep in thought, and possibly denial. She liked Ben and thought he was genuinely trying to help his younger brother stay out of trouble. But he had lied to them. Penny had confirmed Ben was due to shoe her horses on Friday but had cancelled at the last minute, promising to do them on Saturday instead. It could have been Ben in the field.

Kate wanted to believe Ben wouldn't give a drug to a horse with no idea how it might react, but renting that field for the sheep gave him the perfect opportunity to watch the entrance to Clenchers Mill. Richard still couldn't remember what happened that day. What if Ben had been waiting for him? Maybe stopped for a chat and gave the horse a treat along with the pills without Richard even noticing?

If it was Ben, he'd be worried about Richard's memory returning. Could that be why he'd been so quick to apologise for Jade? Were his questions about Richard's recovery more than friendly concerns? When he heard Richard had been discharged from the hospital, did he try to finish him off by disconnecting the brakes? But why single out Richard when it was Alicia's idea to set up a retreat? Unless he had another reason to hate Richard?

Kate opened the kitchen cupboard doors and plonked the ingredients she could find on the side counter. She could create a pasta sauce of sorts from what she had. She doubted anyone would feel much like eating anyway, except for Simon.

Whatever happened, nothing seemed to affect his appetite or his sleep pattern. Taking the apron off its peg, she added his twisted sense of humour to the list of strange attributes. She jumped when the door opened. "I didn't hear you come in."

"Stealth-like. That's me. Like a mountain cat. A useful skill for a private investigator to have," Simon replied. "What are you making? I'm starving."

"Pasta. What did the police say?"

"Not a lot. They wanted to stop by this evening to speak to us. I explained we're taking Helen to visit her parents in hospital, and they've agreed to leave it until tomorrow morning. Did you get hold of the Pearce woman?"

Ignoring the question, Kate asked, "Do you think Ben could have met Richard before he moved into Clencher Mill with Alicia?"

"I doubt it. Ben doesn't appear to be widely travelled, but anything is possible. Why do you think they might have met previously?"

They both turned at the sound of the heavy thud of bags landing on the floor. "I've packed everything I think they might need," Helen said. "When are we leaving for the hospital?"

"Once we've eaten," Simon replied.

Kate pulled out a couple of saucepans from the cupboard next to the sink. "Pasta okay?"

"Sure," Helen said, turning to leave.

"Hang on, a minute," Simon said. "We need to talk about tonight's sleeping arrangements."

Helen shrugged. "I don't know about you guys, but I'm sleeping in my bedroom tonight."

Kate turned around, a can of tomatoes in her hand. "You can't stay in the house by yourself. Do you have any friends or relatives nearby?"

"No, and even if I did, I'm not going anywhere. Someone has to look after the house and the ponies," Helen said, with her arms firmly folded.

"We could do that," Kate said. She had no desire to stay a

moment longer in the cottage, but there was no way she was going to leave Helen to fend for herself. "We could drop you off wherever you like after we leave the hospital."

"I'm staying, here," Helen replied. Looking to Simon for support, she added, "I'm not going to let the bullies win. That's what you said, isn't it?"

Simon looked guiltily from Helen to Kate. Squirming, he said, "Well, yes, but things have changed a little since I said that. I'm not sure how safe it is. I think Kate could be right, and it would be better if you did stay somewhere else. At least until your parents are discharged."

"I'm staying in my home," Helen announced forcibly.

"You can't stay there by yourself," Kate repeated.

Cringing as he watched Kate for a reaction, Simon said, "We could move into the main house." He quickly added, "Just for tonight. It sounds like Alicia will be released from the hospital tomorrow."

Realising she'd been backed into a corner again, Kate turned her back on Simon and poured the tomatoes into a saucepan.

"Kate?"

"We'll ask Alicia where she wants Helen to stay. She might not want any of us in the house," Kate finally said, without turning.

At the hospital, the ward sister insisted on following the, 'two visitors only,' rule. When it was clear she wasn't going to budge, Simon said, "You two go in and sit with Alicia. I'll go and find out what ward Richard is on. I'll meet you back here in an hour."

Simon set off along the corridor, following the directions he'd been given. He marched quickly along, dodging around slow-moving visitors and even slower-moving patients. With his head down, lifting it only occasionally to check he was going the correct way, he overtook several members of the hospital staff.

The smell of disinfectant, the heat, and the squeak his footwear made on the flooring brought back unsettling memories. One of his recurring nightmares involved him running down endless hospital corridors looking for his family after the bombing. His chest tightened, making it difficult to pull in air. He stopped by a water fountain. He braced his arms against the wall and concentrated on controlling his breathing. This wasn't a good time to have a panic attack.

He pressed his forehead against the wall. His legs screamed for permission to run outside while the floor swayed alarmingly beneath his feet. He pushed himself against the wall to maintain his balance as his breathing became painful. He closed his eyes, limiting his thoughts to breathing in and out. Gradually the hallway stopped shifting beneath his feet. He took a drink from the fountain, counted to ten and continued along the corridor towards Richard's ward. By the time he arrived outside and stopped by the hand sanitiser, he felt almost normal.

He spotted Richard in the far bed by the window, before the swing doors had closed behind him. The leg raised in traction was a giveaway. Richard looked deathly white but was awake and alert. Simon raised the bag he was carrying as he approached the bed. "Helen packed a few things she thought you might need. God knows what's in here. It weighs a ton," he said, lowering the bag to the floor.

"Lift it up here," Richard said, patting the side of his bed. "Hopefully, my laptop is in there."

Simon placed the bag on the bed and unzipped it. Richard twisted awkwardly to look inside, wincing in pain. "Let me," Simon said, pulling the laptop from the bag and placing it within easy reach of Richard's good arm.

"Thanks. What else is in there?"

Simon peered inside. "Pyjamas, dressing gown, a book and oh? A bottle of malt whiskey."

"Good girl," Richard said, with a smile. "Pull out the other stuff and hide the bag and whisky in the cabinet over there. There's a good chap."

Simon did as he was told, resisting the urge to say the whiskey probably wasn't allowed. He couldn't see how Richard would be able to retrieve it from the cabinet by himself, anyway.

Richard settled back into his pillows, pain etched on his face with every movement. "I take it Helen and your girlfriend are visiting Alicia, and you drew the short straw to visit me," he joked.

Not bothering to correct him over his relationship with Kate, Simon grinned and replied, "Something like that. How are you feeling?"

"How do you think? I think it's best you leave that warm, fuzzy, caring gig to the girls, don't you? As they're not here, how is Cynthia holding up these days?" Raising his eyebrows at Simon's surprised face, he said, "You'll learn in time, young man. She might be the dragon lady and mad as a box of frogs, but I was married to her for a good few years."

"I'm afraid I don't know. I've been away recently, travelling around Europe. We bumped into her in the pub on our first day back. That's when she asked us to find out what happened with the horse."

"She always did like a few drinks, our Cynthia. Fun at the time, but then I had to put up with the hangovers and the sober times. Still, she wasn't a bad egg. I told Alicia she wouldn't have sent me a dangerous horse. But you know women."

"Indeed." Unable to think of a subtle way to alter the course of the conversation, Simon said, "I wanted to talk to you alone about recent events."

"Oh?"

"The more serious attacks seem to be directed at you, personally. I, I mean we, have started to wonder if these attacks are motivated by something other than the pro-hunting sentiments. Related to your company or other private interests, maybe?"

Richard sank back into his pillows and closed his eyes. Simon looked on waiting for him to respond. Motionless, Richard seemed older. The stubble on his chin was undoubtedly white, and Simon wondered if he dyed his hair. The pressure to keep a woman like Alicia, attractive, younger and, by all accounts, an exceptional designer must weigh heavily at times.

Richard's eyes flicked open. "I think it's unlikely, but what do you want to know?"

Simon pulled his hardbacked chair closer and leaned forward, his hands between his knees. "Can you think of anyone from your business life who would want to harm you?"

Richard laughed. His eyes twinkled in amusement, and the animation returned to his face. "Have you been studying old Columbo movies?"

Simon shifted uncomfortably in his seat. He liked nothing more than to watch those old films on a lazy Sunday afternoon. "No, not at all. It's a relevant question." Gathering his thoughts after the slight that was closer to home than he'd like, he said, "I vaguely remember there was some ugliness a while back. In connection to a London building that you refurbished?"

"Drug addicts and squatters!" Sarcastically, Richard continued, "The poor souls were most offended by being evicted by the legal owners. Heaven knows why the press tried to make it more of an issue than it was. It happens all the time in the bigger cities, especially London." Sighing, he said, "A stink was made about it, but it was years ago. My company was never directly involved in the eviction notices. I doubt it's at all relevant to what's happening now."

"How about your business competitors? I'm guessing competition is fierce for some of the buildings."

"You have been watching too many films. In my game, you win some, and you lose some. If you miss out on the contract for one development, chances are your bid for the next one will be successful. In real life, property development is nowhere near as exciting and cutthroat as you're suggesting. Mostly, it's delays, planning applications and meetings after meetings."

"How about disgruntled ex-employees? Anything like that?"

A frown briefly creased Richard's forehead. "I haven't been directly involved in hiring and firing for years. It's mostly contract-based, and we use an agency for all that."

"You looked like you remembered something earlier?"

"There was a young man. I rather liked him, and we worked together for several years. He was brilliant at sales. He was able to sell ideas and images. We often had flats sold via him before we even started work on them. He had oodles of energy and charisma. The life and soul of any party."

"What happened?"

"We started to get complaints. Women claimed he had behaved inappropriately; others said he turned up to meetings stoned. We stopped using him, eventually." Richard fell silent before adding, "It couldn't be him, though. He died."

"Do you know how?" Simon asked.

"Yes, very sad. I felt I'd judged him too harshly based on reports from other people, without knowing what was going on in his life. He was close to his mother, who was battling cancer. He died of an overdose shortly after she lost her battle. It gave me the final push to make a few personal changes, but I can't see how it could be relevant to these attacks."

"Possibly not, but can you remember his name?"

Richard thought for a while. "Since the accident, my damn memory isn't what it used to be." He patted his laptop balanced on the bed beside him. "I can go through my old records later and let you know."

"If you could, that would be great. I take it you still can't remember the events leading up to the riding accident?"

Richard shook his head. "Can't remember anything about the car accident, either." Running a hand through his hair, he added, "It's blinking annoying. It's a complete blank."

"Concussion will do that," Simon, sympathised. "You can't think of anyone else who might hold a grudge against you? A jealous husband?"

Richard chuckled. "I had opportunities, but I never acted on them. Married to the job for most of my life. There's always only been Cynthia and now Alicia. Sorry to disappoint you on that score." He hesitated before saying, "I've been waiting for the opportunity to speak to you alone. I was dreadfully sorry to hear about your family. They were good people. If there's anything I can do to help you in the future, please let me know."

Simon looked up at the clock at the end of the ward. "Is that the time?" Standing, he said, "Thanks. I should have met up with Kate and Helen ten minutes ago. I hope you feel better soon."

Richard waved him away. "I'll e-mail the name of that guy when I find it."

# CHAPTER TWENTY-FOUR

Helen gave in to exhaustion around one o'clock and went up to bed. Simon collected a beer from the fridge and settled in the armchair in the living room.

Kate walked in with a glass of red wine. "This house is beautiful, but I feel even more out of place here than I did in the cottage. On top of the attacks, it's like I've walked in on the double feature in *Homes and Gardens*. I'm too scared to touch anything in case I move it slightly out of place," she said, taking a seat and placing her glass carefully on a coaster on the coffee table.

Simon twisted to face her, with his legs dangling over the side of the chair. "I don't know. This is the most comfortable chair. I hate it when furniture is designed to look good, rather than for comfort." Swinging his legs to the front and reclining back, he said, "How did it go with the Pearce woman? You avoided answering before."

Kate sighed. "Her name is Penny, and Ben was booked to shoe her horses on Friday. Only, he cancelled at the last minute."

"He lied, in other words. He could have been the unknown walker in the field," Simon said.

"It may not have been on purpose. He was going on what his phone calendar said. It could simply be he hadn't changed the entry, and he forgot."

"And pigs might fly. We know what his opinion of Richard and Alicia is. I've already given his name to the police. I'll let them know tomorrow that he gave us a false alibi."

"I'm sure they'll work it out for themselves." After taking a sip of her wine, Kate said, "I don't think he's the type of person who would harm an animal on purpose. Or creep around at night tampering with cars. I gained the impression he's someone decent and reasonable. Not the type who would try to kill a stranger because they disagreed with his viewpoint."

"And, of course, he's rather good-looking," Simon said.

"Irrelevant," Kate replied, wearily. She finished her wine and took the empty glass back to the kitchen. "I'm turning in for the night. You won't forget to switch the alarms on before you go to bed?"

Simon pulled the handwritten sheet of paper from his pocket. "I've got all the codes here. Go and get some sleep. I'll be up soon."

By three o'clock, Kate accepted she was not going to get back to sleep. Wriggling into her dressing gown, she crossed the room and pulled back the heavy blackout curtains. A full moon cast a silvery hue across the rear garden. There was just enough light to highlight all the hedges and bushes an intruder could hide behind. She tiptoed past the closed bedroom doors and felt her way along the hall to the staircase without turning on the lights. Downstairs, the huge entrance hall window let in enough moonlight for her to see her way into the living room.

She stopped abruptly behind a sofa, transfixed by the sliver of artificial light shining under the kitchen door. With a pounding heart and a dry mouth, she walked backwards across the living room to the two swords, displayed crisscrossed on the wall. She had no idea whether they were genuine antiques or replicas. Pulling one from its protective sheaf, it looked sharp enough to do some damage, either way. She hesitated before returning upstairs to ring the police and wake Simon.

Dithering in the middle of the room, she heard Simon's voice coming from the kitchen. She hadn't realised she'd been holding her breath. Gasping for air, she quietly replaced the sword in its rightful place.

In the kitchen, Simon was pacing while listening to someone on the phone. He held out his hand to silence Kate when she entered. Kate rubbed her eyes and glanced at the open laptop on the table and the clock on the wall, before spotting the pot of coffee on the side counter. Simon continued to pace, occasionally nodding his head and mumbling an acknowledgement to whoever was on the other end of the phone.

Kate poured herself a coffee and took a seat to wait. Phone calls at three in the morning meant something serious had happened. The phone ringing and Simon running down to answer it, could have been what woke her.

Simon ended the call and poured himself a fresh coffee. He sat staring at his laptop screen in silence, while Kate itched with apprehension. "What was that about? What's happened?"

Simon looked through her with glazed eyes, his thoughts miles away. "Sorry, what did you say?"

Kate frowned. She'd never seen Simon look so spaced out. Wondering if he was sleepwalking, she racked her brain, trying to remember what she should do. She was positive she'd read somewhere waking a sleepwalker was dangerous. Tentatively, she asked, "Are you okay?"

Simon's eyes gradually focused on Kate, and he came out of his trance. "Tired, but yes, I'm okay."

Noticing Simon was wearing the same clothes as the day before, she asked, "Did you fall asleep in the chair? I think you'd better go upstairs and get some sleep."

Simon rubbed his hands up and down his face. The whites of his eyes were bloodshot. He took a slurp of coffee, turned his attention towards his laptop and said, "I will in a minute."

"What have you been doing all night? And who was that on the phone?"

"I was trying to decide whether to tell the police about Harry and Jade, so I looked at their Facebook profiles. Harry has about twenty friends and barely uses it. Jade is slightly more active.

She has a few more friends, although they all appear to be either family members or hunt supporters. Her profile picture is a cartoon figure, and although she posts very little to her page, she regularly posts in several pro-hunt groups she's a member of."

"Okay," Kate said, when Simon looked up at her, expecting a response.

"Then, I looked at the account Jade used to befriend Bradley, the boy who killed himself. It was a basic fake account made up of stock photographs. It wouldn't have stood up to any serious scrutiny. If the police had carried out any sort of investigation into Bradley's online activities, they would have traced her, even if Bradley deleted everything at his end. I pulled up the newspaper reports on his death. He'd had a run-in with a group of girls over his hunting activities during morning break. He hung himself in the school toilets during the lunch hour. Once a connection between the school bullying was made, no other investigations were carried out. Interestingly, all five girls were shocked anything they said could have led to suicide."

"They would say that, wouldn't they?"

Simon held up one of the two phones, lying on the table. "Except we know Jade sent him a text just before twelve o'clock that day. If the police hadn't jumped to the conclusion that Bradley killed himself because of the girls taunting him that day they would have been on to Jade and Harry very quickly."

"The police made an obvious mistake," Kate said. "If they hadn't, it would have come out about Helen and Alicia."

Simon put the other phone on the table. "I then looked at the Facebook account they used to trick Helen and Alicia. That's where it gets interesting. That account is far more sophisticated and would fool most people. It runs back to 2015 and shows all the usual posts and photographs you'd expect on a teenager's account. All in chronological order showing the same boy growing up. I phoned a friend who knows about these things. He confirmed it took some skill to create the account. He's going to go deeper to find out who set it up."

"You rang him at three in the morning?" Kate asked,

incredulously.

"He sleeps all day and is online all night. Oh, and one final thing. How did they get Alicia's mobile number? Which of them do you think is clever enough to do that?"

"When she contacted Ben about the sheep being loose?"

"The texts pre-date that by a long way," Simon said. "There's a third person involved here. I'm sure of it. Someone clever and determined was in the background, manipulating Harry and Jade to do their dirty work."

"That decides it. You have to give this to the police, regardless of what you've promised Alicia and Helen." Kate looked up at the kitchen clock. "Who'll be arriving in less than five hours."

Simon closed the laptop lid. "So long as I can tell them when Helen is not in earshot. I don't want her thinking I've betrayed her." He stood and stretched his back. Picking up the laptop, he said, "Meanwhile, I'm going up to get some sleep."

# CHAPTER
# TWENTY-FIVE

Kate opened the front door to the two, uniformed officers and invited them inside. Kate had expected a more senior, plain-clothed detective rather than two constables who didn't fill her with any confidence. They appeared over-awed by the grandeur of the house. She fleetingly wondered if she'd looked as wide-eyed on her first night. The meal on the patio now seemed like it had happened months ago.

Kate led them into the kitchen, where Helen jumped up from nervously biting her nails, and asked, "Any news on my parents?"

Kate registered that was the first time Helen had referred to Richard as her parent. A slip of the tongue? The drama of the last few days had created an unusual bond, and she felt protective towards Helen. So protective, she worried about leaving Helen alone with the constables while she woke Simon.

The taller of the two constables, replied, "We haven't heard anything more since yesterday."

Kate made a pot of coffee while the constables seated themselves around the table.

"Your parents should make a full recovery and will be home before you know it," the shorter constable called Oliver Price said. He pulled out a notepad from his breast pocket. "There are signs the car they were travelling in had been tampered with." Looking down at his notebook, he said, "I spoke to a Simon Morris, yesterday. He suggested there have been other recent incidents of concern. Is he here?"

Kate placed five mugs on the table along with the pot of freshly made coffee, a jug of cream and a sugar bowl. Sliding into the seat at the head of the table, she said, "He's upstairs sleeping after rather a late night. I'll go and wake him in a minute. Please help yourself to coffee, and we'll try to answer your questions."

Stirring sugar into his coffee, Price said, "Perhaps you could describe some of these incidents of concern."

Helen stared miserably at the table, so Kate told them about Paddy being drugged, and the vandalism to the gate, Alicia's car and the garage doors.

Price dutifully wrote everything down, and said, "I'll fill in a report when we get back to the station. I can't promise anything, but I'll speak to my senior officer about this."

Kate thanked him and indicated she had more to tell him. She waited for him to flick over the page of his notepad before continuing. Feeling guilty about what she was going to say, she spoke faster than normal. "It will be in the police report, I'm sure, but a Mark Oates, who arrived shortly after Richard was thrown from his horse, caught sight of someone walking away across the adjacent field. The sheep in the field belong to Ben Teobald. When we asked him if he was there that day, tending to his sheep, he claimed he wasn't and gave a false alibi. We've since learnt he has strong views on "outsiders" moving into the area and anti-blood sports protesters generally."

Price finally looked up from scribbling on his pad. "I will pass all of this on. Is there anything else you'd like to add?"

Kate glanced across at Helen before shaking her head. "Should I wake Simon now?"

Price replied, "Will he be able to tell us much more?"

Kate looked over at Helen again, and replied, "Possibly. I'm not sure."

The constables stood. "Thank you for the coffee. Your friend can ring the station if he wishes to add anything. He should ask for Detective Collins, who I'll be speaking to about all this or me. Detective Collins was called out to a missing person case earlier this morning. Otherwise, he would have been here now."

Kate saw them to the door and returned to the kitchen. "Let's hope Detective Collins has some idea what he's doing," she said to Helen.

Helen snorted her contempt. "That was a complete waste of time."

Kate dropped onto a chair. "If we don't hear from this detective in a couple of hours, I'll ring him."

Helen remained silent. Pale and drawn, she kept her head down as she dug her fingernails into the coaster. Kate squeezed her shoulder as she passed her, taking the empty mugs to the draining board. A girl of her age shouldn't have dark rings around her eyes unless it was the morning after a good night. Helen looked a picture of total misery. Leaning against the counter, Kate said, "I don't know about you, but I need to get out of this place for a few hours. How about we head into town and hit the shopping malls?"

In a monotone, Helen replied, "You go. I need to stick around here in case the hospital rings. If they don't discharge Mum today, I'll go and visit her. You take the car. I can call a taxi."

"There are such things as mobile phones," Kate said, and immediately regretted it. "What I meant is, if the hospital rings, we can cut our shopping short and get straight over there. Why don't I ring them now to check they have my mobile number? Or maybe there's no need. If they ring here, Simon can let us know."

Helen shifted in her seat. Wearily, she said, "The shopping mall is over an hour's drive from the hospital. Don't let me stop you. You go."

Kate slumped back onto a kitchen chair. Helen's mood was bringing hers down. She had to get out of the house before she went crazy, and she was determined she was taking Helen with her. She'd prefer to be somewhere miles away, but she appreciated why Helen didn't want to roam too far. "Do you ride? How about we take the horses out?"

"The ponies are too old to be ridden. Mum saved them from some local sanctuary. I'm pretty sure it was part of the agreement they are never to be ridden. Even by small children on lead reins."

Moping around the house wasn't going to do any of them any good. Not to be defeated, Kate asked, "Is there anything local you'd like to see or do? We'll keep our phones on so we can drive to the hospital at a moment's notice."

Albert shuffled towards Helen from his basket and rested his head on her lap. Absentmindedly, Helen stroked the dog's ears. Albert nudged his head further into her lap, demanding more attention. Looking down at the dog, Helen finally said, "It sounds a bit lame, but we could drive the dogs out to the Valley Park for a walk. I went there with Mum last month. If I can find it again, there's a trail through the woods that's peaceful."

"That sounds like a splendid idea," Kate said, silently thanking Albert. "I'll grab my walking boots and leave a message for Simon, so he knows where we are."

"It's a ten-minute drive from here. And the car park charges. Not a lot. I think it's only a couple of quid," Helen said.

I'll grab some change with my boots," Kate said, heading towards the door. "Do you need to take anything?"

Helen put both hands on the table and slowly pushed back to stand. "My boots are in the hall."

Simon appeared in the doorway, making Kate jump. Tufts of his hair stuck up in strange angles, and he looked half-asleep. "Why didn't you wake me?" he grumbled, as he stumbled into the kitchen. He dropped heavily onto a chair and held his head in his hands. "My head is killing me."

Helen opened a kitchen drawer and placed a blister pack of painkillers on the table. "I'll get you a glass of water."

While Helen was at the sink, Kate explained about the two constables and gave him Detective Collins' details. "We're going to a local park to get some fresh air with the dogs. Do you want to join us?"

Simon gratefully took the glass from Helen and popped two painkillers from the packet. "No, you two go and enjoy yourself. The dogs will appreciate a good run. I have a couple of things I'd like to follow up on."

Helen left to get her boots while Kate wiped the table. "I was going to take the Mini, will that be a problem?"

"No worries. I'll use the camper van if I need to go anywhere. It could do with being started up. After all the miles we travelled across Europe, it's probably feeling very neglected. Where are you headed?"

"The Valley Park. I've not heard of it. It was Helen's idea." Kate laughed. "Or possibly Albert's. He managed to cheer Helen up when I failed. She doesn't want to stray too far in case the hospital calls. Which reminds me, I'm going to ring them to give them my mobile number, but if they should ring here, will you contact me?"

"If I'm here, yes. While you're gone, I'm hoping to speak to Detective Collins. Did you tell them Ben lied about his whereabouts?"

"Yes." Checking Helen wasn't returning, Kate quickly added, "I didn't get the chance to say anything about the blackmail."

"Leave it with me. I'm going to pay Harry and Jade a visit later to find out who set up that Facebook page for them."

"Why don't you leave it to the police?" Kate asked.

"If I find out something more, I'll pass it over to their capable hands."

"You're sure you're okay about us taking the dogs and leaving you here by yourself?"

"Yes! Go! They'll enjoy it," Simon said.

He slipped down in his seat as he watched Kate, Helen and the dogs cross the car park to the entrance to the park. He'd been in two minds whether to follow them or to deal with Simon first. Their choice of destination was a good sign. It was an area he knew well, and mobile phone reception was sketchy. Large areas of the park had no reception at all, especially through the wooded areas.

He locked his car and headed across the car park. Keeping an eye on the two women, he dropped down by the mini, pretending to tie his shoelaces. Checking there was no one nearby, he pulled the knife from his pocket and dug it deep into the two rear car tyres. Now he had options. Plan one was to catch them off guard in a secluded area. Plan two was to notice their distress when they discovered the car tyres and offer to drive them either home or to pick up a spare tyre.

No one took any notice of him, paying his admission and strolling into the park. Why would they? His age, dress and appearance screamed standard National Trust visitor.

At night, he became someone else. He'd been fascinated with computers from the start when they were heavy, noisy and slow. Not for the stupid games and social media sites, others seemed so impressed with. He was interested in how they worked and in developing his own programmes. His hobby had grown into an obsession during Betty's fight with cancer. His salvation, when she finally lost her battle. By then, he was deep inside the dark web, and the art of hacking and becoming anonymous had become second nature. Within the groups, members used nicknames, and no one revealed their true identities. Occasionally, he'd accidentally let slip a few false details, such as hangovers after a night of clubbing or drop hints that he'd met a girl. Things that suggested he was a young man in his twenties.

His online community was international but incredibly select. Only excellence gave them an in to the group. He'd covered all his tracks when he'd contacted the two country bumpkins and created the account for their crude use of technology. He had set traps so he would be alerted if someone of any talent tried to unravel what he'd done. He wasn't surprised the attempted breach was by someone he was already connected with. It hadn't taken long for him to discover who their mutual acquaintance was. A funny old world. Everyone is interconnected whether they realise it or not.

He smiled when he saw the direction Kate and Helen were taking. He knew that pathway well. It had long, secluded stretches where there was no telephone signal at all. On a weekday morning, there weren't many people around. Those that were milling about looked just like him. People seeking peace and solitude were unlikely to take a path someone else had chosen.

# CHAPTER TWENTY-SIX

After two coffees, the painkillers were kicking in. Gone were the days when Simon could pull an all-nighter with few ill effects. It hadn't been his first night without sleep. He hadn't wanted Kate to be any more anxious than she already was, so he'd kept it from her that underneath his bravado, his own deep feeling of unease had been keeping him awake at night. As the one who insisted they stay, he had used his insomnia wisely, keeping a watchful eye for any unwanted intruders from his bedroom window each evening. Now he was paying the price.

He opened his laptop and flicked through the Facebook page Harry had used. A pointless exercise, as he'd already tried everything he knew to try to work out how it had been set up and backdated. Ever the optimist, he scrolled up and down in the vague hope that something he'd missed on every other search would leap out at him. Occasionally, good things do happen. There was no point ringing his friend. At eleven in the morning, he'd be fast asleep.

Leaving the programme running, he telephoned the local police and asked to speak to Detective Collins. A blunt, bored-sounding woman took his details and robotically said the detective would get back to him. Despite being his most charming self, all he achieved was her promise she wouldn't go home when her shift finished in a couple of hours without passing on his message.

Simon tapped through a few screens before closing his laptop down. It felt strange not to have the dogs jumping around his feet when he laced his boots. Closing the door without promising them he wouldn't be long, created a heavy sadness. Without Kate, he was the male equivalent of a crazy cat lady, only with dogs.

He drove on autopilot to Harry's home, thinking about Kate, while hoping that Harry would be in and his older brother out working. The thatched farmhouse nestled at the bottom of the hill came into sight earlier than he remembered from his last visit. In the dark, it had been an unremarkable oblong building. In daylight, the rounded, thick walls smoothed over time by the elements and covered with a rambling, red rose looked solid and inviting. The freshly painted front door was covered by a trellis porch. It was hard to tell where the wood ended, and the rose bush began. Someone took a great deal of time keeping it pruned and tidy.

A smiling woman in an apron, wiping her red hands on a towel, opened the door. Simon stuck his hand out. "Hello, Mrs. Teobald. I came around the other night to carry out some repairs on Harry's laptop. Is he around?"

"Oh, yes. Arthur mentioned it. I was at the WI meeting. Is there still a problem? Harry needs it in good working order. He's applying to go to the Agricultural College."

"I need to check a couple of things are still running okay. All part of my after-care service. Is he in?"

"Sorry, yes. What am I like? Come in."

Simon followed her along a narrow corridor. The uneven floor caused him to knock his shoulders on the walls. It led into a bright airy kitchen painted a cheery yellow. On the sturdy kitchen table that dominated the centre of the room was a mountain of potatoes.

"I'm preparing for the village fete this weekend," Harry's mother explained. "Are you going? It's always a fun event with lots to do." Jovially rolling her eyes, she added, "The beer tent usually does the best trade."

"I'm not sure. Maybe."

"Anyhow, it's Harry you want to see, not me." She opened the far door which led into the rear garden. "He's out there, mowing the lawn for me. He's such a good boy. Once he gets to college, I expect he'll still try to find the time to help me out."

Simon nodded as he edged out through the door. If only she knew what the little sod got up to. She wouldn't be so full of praise, then. Or would she dismiss it, claiming others had led her little darling astray?

The spacious, green lawn sloped gently away from the house down to an orchard. Harry was driving a sit-on mower along the bottom of the garden. Simon waved and stood at the top, waiting for him to come up. Harry meticulously drove a circuit of the lawn before stopping the mower a few feet away. He leaned back in the seat and lit a cigarette. "What do you want, now?" he snarled.

Harry's mother called from the open kitchen window. "Do you boys want some lemonade?"

Harry smiled back. "No, thank you. We're fine," he replied, politely.

Simon turned around as her head disappeared back into the kitchen. Turning back to Harry, he said, "A lovely lady. I expect she'd be very disappointed if she knew about what you've been up to."

Harry pulled hard on his cigarette, avoiding eye contact. Simon had clearly hit a nerve. Whatever he was in the outside world, at home, he was Mummy's little soldier. He would probably do anything to retain his mother's approval. "Give me the name of the person who set up the fake Facebook account you used to trick Helen, and I'll leave you alone. Does that sound like a good deal? Or would you prefer to see much more of me? Your mother has taken rather a shine to me."

Concentrating on blowing smoke rings, Harry replied, "No idea what you're talking about?"

"I think you do. There's no way you or Jade set up that account. And how did you get hold of Alicia's mobile number?" When Harry remained silent, Simon added, "Pity you won't give me the name." Turning towards the house, he said, "I wonder if I showed your mother what's on your phone if she would remember your friend's name."

"No! Wait!" Harry said. He lifted a leg and stubbed his cigarette out on the sole of his shoe. "I can't tell you who he is, because I don't know. He contacted Jade online. Funny thing is, she's tried since to get up his details, and they've disappeared. Honestly, we have no idea who he is." With pleading eyes, he said, "Please, don't tell my mum. I've already promised I'll never do anything like it again. I'm applying to go to Agricultural College and everything."

"Any idea where I'll find Jade at this time of the day?"

"It won't do you any good. She doesn't know anything more than I do. She freaked out when everything from him disappeared."

"She could still tell me how he made contact with her to start with."

"I can tell you that. Online, via some Facebook group, she's in. Only he's not a member anymore. I told you. Everything has disappeared," Harry said.

"I'd still like to speak to her."

"You could try ringing her. Oh, of course, you can't," Harry said. "You've got our phones."

"Do you have her home number?" Simon asked.

Harry shook his head. "I only used her mobile. Her dad can get quite nasty. Her mum isn't much better, to be fair, once she's had a drink. You're a braver man than me if you do, but you could go to her house. I can't help you more than that. We've broken up. It's probably for the best. Anvil's happy now."

"Any reason why you split?"

"I want to make something of my life." Harry stared across the half-mown lawn. "I need to get on and finish this." When Simon didn't turn to leave, Harry added, "If you must know. I didn't know she was still texting that kid. She said she'd stopped. The newspapers said he was bullied at school, and that's why he did it, so I believed her."

Simon believed Harry was genuinely sorry, and he wanted to

turn his life around. Maybe, one day he would be a responsible adult. He had the support of a family that cared. While it was a part of that process, he was disappointed he had dumped Jade so abruptly. If she hadn't been so unpleasant, he'd almost feel sorry for her.

Taking in the farmhouse grounds, he wondered how much Jade had meant to Harry and how much influence she had over him if he was prepared to give her up so easily. Was she just someone fun at the time, but not quite marriage material? Maybe Kate did have a point. When you're a kid, social status means nothing. But as you age, people often conform to their peer group. He had to prove to Kate, he wasn't like that.

"Before I go, are you sure you had nothing to do with drugging Richard's horse, and you weren't in the field tending to your sheep the day he fell from the horse?"

"No way! I've told you before that I would never do anything like that. I was in the pub. You can check."

"It's not a great distance between the field and the pub. If you ran, you could have made it before the air ambulance flew over."

"I swear to God, I didn't. I was there from opening time."

Watching Harry closely, Simon was convinced Harry was telling the truth. "If I ever find out you've lied, I will hand your phone to the police." After a brief pause to allow the threat to sink in, he asked, "How about glueing the gates and the dead crows?"

Harry didn't respond, but before he turned away, Simon noticed a slight facial twitch. "Harry! This is important. Did you or Jade have anything to do with the gate? I won't tell anyone, provided you tell me the truth now."

Looking at the ground, Harry mumbled, "Jade thought it would be funny."

"Hilarious," Simon said, dryly. "And did you come back a few nights later to leave a dead fox on the car seat and break into the garage?"

Harry raised his head in surprise. Maintaining eye contact, he shook his head, and replied, "No. That's nothing to do with us."

"Would Jade have gone back by herself and done it?"

Harry thought for a while, before replying, "I don't think so. Which night was it?" When Simon confirmed it was Tuesday at about two o'clock at night, Harry added, "Then no. Jade was drunk that night and slept it off here. Anything else you want to accuse us of?"

"That's it for now. I'll see you around," Simon said, walking away with his hands shoved in his pockets and the sound of the mower starting up ringing in his ears.

# CHAPTER TWENTY-SEVEN

Simon drove to the other side of the village where Jade lived. In daylight, he could see how overgrown and unkempt the front garden was. Typical of the social housing built at the end of the war the house was well-proportioned and the garden three times the size allocated to modern new-builds. Potentially, it could be a lovely home. Currently, it looked as untidy and neglected on the outside as it had on the inside.

Jade's father opened the door in jeans and a torn T-shirt. "Yes?" he said, impatiently.

"I was looking for Jade?"

Her father looked him up and down twice. "She ain't in," he said, and promptly slammed the door shut.

Simon sat in the front seat of the camper van and called the local police station to be told by the same bored voice as earlier that Detective Collins remained unavailable. He started the engine and headed back to Clenchers Mill.

Once there, Simon settled himself at the kitchen table and switched on the laptop. Richard hadn't e-mailed the name of the young man who had died of an overdose following the death of his mother. He wondered if he could find it himself. He might come across something else of interest if he dug around Richard's business interests a little.

He started with the company's official website and rang the contact number given for general enquiries. He managed to charm his way through to the Personnel Department, where he ran out of luck as he half anticipated. No one was prepared to hand out details of ex-employees or individual agents, even if they were dead.

His next step was to pull up all the business and media reports, he could find. Once he was on the right track, he discovered numerous reports and photographs of not only the buildings but also the teams of people involved in Richard's property ventures. Flicking through them, there was a depressing number of well-groomed, good-looking, suited men of roughly the right age. Without a name, it was impossible to work out which of them was the one Richard had referred to.

Along with the positive promotional press releases, Simon found several negative press stories. Emotive tales of short-notice evictions and broken promises of the inclusion of affordable properties within the new designs. He knew Richard bought rundown blocks of flats and turned them into expensive sought-after apartments, but he had no idea of how brutally it was done. Whatever Richard claimed, many of these displaced people would have an axe to grind, and it only took one to be savvy enough to discover Richard was the man profiting from their hardship. Simon jotted down a list of names of the people who had been most aggressive in voicing their complaints to the press.

He almost missed a small report, which described how in one of his ventures, a fluid number of twenty to thirty long-term squatters had been physically forced from the building. In the scuffle, one nameless man had been killed. Despite several attempts, the young man's identity had never been discovered. Simon leaned back in his chair. He doubted the authorities were as exhaustive in their enquiries as they claimed. Their interest in tracing an unemployed, homeless man would have been minimal to start with and dwindled to nothing within a few days. For a family missing a son, things would be very different. He jotted down the name of the reporter as something to follow up on.

Before contacting the reporter, Simon rang Cynthia. Once general pleasantries were gone through, he asked her if she remembered the name of one of Richard's business associates who had died of an overdose.

"I do remember something about that. I always wondered if there was more to it. Richard was deeply upset by it. More than upset. Shaken, maybe. We were going to attend the funeral together, but Richard felt unwell, so we stayed away. He sent someone else to represent the company, and I believe there was an uncomfortable moment where the father draped himself over the coffin, wailing. Friends had to pull him away."

"Do you remember his name?"

"Now, let me think."

Simon held his breath while impatiently waiting for a name.

After a prolonged silence, Cynthia said, "Hang on. I keep all my diaries. His name should be in there."

Simon crossed his legs, bouncing the top foot while listening to the silence. He was tempted to hang up and call the reporter instead. On reflection, death during an eviction was a stronger motive for revenge than an overdose brought on by the death of a parent. That was where he should concentrate his efforts.

Finally, Cynthia reappeared on the line. "Here we are. The service was held in Saint John's church in Surrey. The young man's name was David Oates."

Simon spluttered, "Thank you, Cynthia," and hung up. Could it be a coincidence that a Mark Oates happened to be in the lane when Richard's horse had gone crazy? The Mark they met appeared kind and laid-back. He'd also called an ambulance for Richard. His wife was alive, wasn't she? He thought back over the conversation they'd had with him. He couldn't recall Mark referring to his wife in the present tense.

Simon broke out into a cold sweat, and his mouth went dry. Mark also had expensive laptops and a good-looking, dark-haired son who died of a drug overdose. Simon recalled the conversation in Mark's living room. He'd sounded sad when he told them about his son, but also bitter and angry. Did Mark think Richard had gotten his son hooked on drugs? That was crazy. Richard liked his brandy and whiskey, but Simon couldn't remember the vaguest of hints connecting him with drugs.

Simon closed his eyes, trying to conjure up the photograph in Mark's living room he'd briefly seen. He scrunched his eyes tighter and pressed his forefingers into his temples to no avail. The cursory glance he'd given the photograph hadn't been enough to create a recoverable image.

His decision on what to do next was interrupted by his mobile's ringtone. Scrambling to answer it, with his mind elsewhere, he knocked the phone to the floor. The screen cracked, but it continued to ring. He snatched it up, and curtly said, "Hello."

"Hello. Simon Morris? I'm Detective Collins. I've been asked to contact you."

All previous thoughts of what he was going to say disappeared, along with any logical ones. "It's Mark Oates! Mark Oates has been trying to kill Richard and intimidate his family. Because his son died of an overdose. I know where he lives. Lilac cottage in Somerbus. You can go and arrest him. There's bound to be some incriminating evidence there."

"Hold your horses," Collins said. "Slow down and start at the beginning. The message I have here, says you want me to arrest Ben Teobald. Which one is it?"

Simon rushed through everything that happened since their arrival at Clenchers Mill, minus the online blackmail. He reasoned that bringing Harry and Jade into the mix would only muddy the waters. Instead, he went on to explain what he'd discovered about David Oates."

Detective Collins remained silent until Simon had finished. In a slow, drawn-out accent, he said, "That all sounds very suspicious, but it could be as innocent as the reported disappearance of a local woman, I've wasted most of my day on. Neither the horse incident nor the vandalism has been reported to us. Without a recorded crime, we've nothing to go on other than your word."

"It all happened! What about the tampering of the car? You have got evidence of that. I don't think this guy will stop until he's finally killed, Richard. He needs to be arrested," Simon insisted. "He could be at the hospital now, planning another attack."

"Calm down, son, and let me finish. We've not received complaints about anything else, but I agree there is clear evidence the brakes on Mr Fielding's car were tampered with."

"So, you can arrest him."

"I can't go around arresting people for no good reason. What I'll do is this. I'll drive over to you now to take a statement. Then, we can go from there."

"What about Richard and Alicia? They're sitting ducks in the hospital. Can they be given some protection?"

"I'll decide that after I've taken your statement and spoken to Mark Oates," Collins said, chuckling to himself.

"Well, hurry up. Please," Simon said sharply, not happy that the detective found his concerns so humorous. He wouldn't find it so funny when Simon handed him solid evidence showing he was right to be so concerned. But first, he had to find that evidence.

Simon returned to his laptop. He pushed the mouse around the screen, bringing up the different articles, willing himself to recognise David Oates among the group photographs of smiling people. After a while, they didn't look normal anymore. The faces distorted and jeered at him, their false grins hiding their killer instincts. His brain whirled into overdrive, dreaming up unpleasant scenarios of what would happen next. It refused to focus on the smaller details. He pushed himself away from the table and started to pace. Every nerve in his body, full of frustrated energy, begged for some direction. Checking the time repeatedly, he considered running around the grounds. Kate swore it soothed her frayed nerves when the world was closing in on her.

He picked up his phone and unlocked the cracked screen. Would there be someone more senior to Collins at the station? The more he thought about their telephone conversation, the less confidence he had in the man. If he could convince someone of the seriousness of the situation, the matter could be passed to a larger station. One with a team of detectives who dealt with serious crime daily rather than spending their time rounding up escaped cattle. What if Mark was at the hospital now? Strangling the life out of Richard while he sat in his kitchen drinking coffee.

He jumped when the phone sprang to life in his hands. An unknown number flashed up on the screen. "Hello?" He sagged in relief and crumpled onto a chair when the caller informed him, they were calling from the hospital. The colour drained from his face, and he sat bolt upright. "What do you mean you can't get hold of Kate? She rang and gave you her number, didn't she?" His brain came up with a million reasons why Kate wasn't answering. "The reception is lousy in some areas. Yes. Leave it with me. I'll continue to try to get a hold of her. If I can't, I'll come and collect Alicia."

He paced as he continually hit re-dial. Kate said they were going to some parkland with the dogs. The Valley Park, that was it. He walked back to the laptop to google the name. Frowning at the images of forest walkways, he drummed his fingers on the table. It explained the lack of signal, but they had been expecting a call. Hadn't Helen insisted they didn't go too far in case the hospital called?

He grabbed the keys to the camper van and slipped on his hiking boots. Tying the laces in the hall, he heard the crunch of tyres outside on the driveway. He opened the front door, hoping to see Alicia's mini.

Instead, an overweight man heaved himself out of a Vauxhall Astra. The car's suspension bounced the car level once he stood. He raised a hand in greeting. "Hi! I'm Detective Collins. We spoke on the phone."

# CHAPTER TWENTY-EIGHT

The more miles she put between herself and Clenchers Mill, the more relaxed Kate felt. Living the last few days on high alert had been exhausting. The cottage was beautiful, but there was an underlying sinister feel to the building that set her teeth on edge. Ghost stories had always spooked her, and it had crossed her mind several times to research the history of Clenchers Mill. There might be an additional reason for her feeling of unease other than the recent attacks on the family.

She wound the window down and willed her tension to blow away. Smiling across at Helen, she sensed the girl was equally relieved to get away from the place. Even if it was for only a few hours. Helen looked younger with her loosened hair flying about her face from the open window. She still checked her phone screen every five minutes, but that was understandable in the circumstances.

"I doubt the hospital will ring until lunchtime at the earliest," Kate said. "If you're worried you can ring them, but the nurse told me they both had a comfortable night."

"Yeah, you said," Helen replied, slipping the phone back into her pocket. "Force of habit, I guess. What do you think will happen now?"

"I'm not sure. The police will fully investigate, I guess."

"Someone must have played about with brakes," Helen said. "Richard is anal about car maintenance. He's always tinkering in the garage and nagging mum about keeping the mini fully serviced. He is that man, who checks the oil and tyre pressure every week and walks once around a car before getting in."

"The police will get to the bottom of it," Kate reassured Helen. "How about we forget all the bad stuff that's gone on this week? Just for an hour?"

"Easier said than done, but I'll try," Helen replied.

Driving along the twisty lane towards the park car park, Kate smiled to herself as she sensed Helen fighting an inner battle not to re-look at her phone. Kate always kept her phone charged and with her, but she'd never become obsessed with social media. Many of her friends fell into the trap of being more concerned about how their life looked to outsiders than actually living it. She wasn't surprised some people viewed it like any other addiction. It had been liberating to go off-grid travelling across Europe with Simon without feeling the need to post pictures of every single stop.

The first few rows in the car park were already filled, and Kate glanced towards a coach spilling out primary school children next to the main entrance. "Whatever direction they take. We'll go in the opposite direction."

Helen high-fived her. "Agreed."

They picked up a map from outside the gift shop and moved to the side to study it. It took ages for the adults to organise the children into smaller groups and decide where they were heading. Kate and Helen laughed as they turned simultaneously to walk in the opposite direction. Helen continued to study the map and showed Kate a circular walk that should take a little over an hour. Once they were on the path, they released the dogs from their leads, and they both ran ahead sniffing at the ground.

Other than the one boisterous group of children, the park was peaceful. Lively chatter had floated out from the gift shop and café, but there were only a handful of people walking the trails. There was no one in front or behind them as they followed the path deeper into the woods. The only clue they weren't in the middle of nowhere was the occasional park bench.

Helen made an effort to stop worrying and checking her phone every five minutes. She slipped it into her pocket and chattered happily about her plans to take environmental studies at university and how she had attended recent demonstrations in London, with Alicia's full support.

Kate thought back to her teenage years. Politics and protests had never played a part in her school days, and she was impressed with how enlightened Helen's generation was. One of the only benefits of social media. People now received information from a wealth of different sources online. The level of fake news was probably no higher than previously, only before it was tightly controlled by the government. Now, anyone with a phone could post stories as they happened. It was just a shame that some used the technology to distort the truth. While others, as Alicia and Helen had learned, used it in other devious ways.

Kate felt a sudden dig in the ribs. Helen said, laughing, "Hey! You're miles away."

"Sorry, I was rather. My mind wanders all over the place while I'm walking."

"My dad's the same. He spends most of his time in a dream world," Helen said.

"Do you see much of him?" Kate asked, realising she knew nothing about Alicia's first husband.

"I see him a couple of times a month."

"Don't be angry with me for asking this question. But is it possible your dad has anything to do with the attacks on Richard?"

Helen laughed out loud. "Dad! No. For one thing, he's as happy as Larry with his girlfriend and her two kids. He's more of a passive observer of life than someone likely to take action. As long as he has his Sunday paper and spends the afternoon in the pub with his mates, he's happy with his lot. Mum will tell you. They drifted into a relationship and had me and then drifted out of the relationship. There was never any animosity between them, even when they first split up."

"That must make things much easier for you," Kate said, making a mental note to check Helen's father was as relaxed with the situation, as she suggested.

"It does, although I can't imagine what they ever had in common. Even I get frustrated with his laid-back approach to life. If it says it's true in the Daily Mail, then it must be true, is the extent of dad's intellectual consideration of the world. Whereas mum. Well, she questions everything. She's pretty cool really, but don't tell her I said that. Things have been difficult recently, and we have had arguments, but she's open to new ideas and does listen to my viewpoint. That's more than most of my friends' parents do."

Kate was eager to catch up with the dogs that had disappeared out of sight around a bend in the track while they'd been chatting. Relieved to see them a short distance ahead, she pointed out the roof of a small building to their right and said, "That would be a great place to have a café or bar. I'm about ready for a break. How much further until this path starts to turn back on itself. We've been walking for quite some time."

Helen pulled out the map. Frowning, she said, "I think we should have taken the other path a while back where it forked. It might be best we turn around?"

"Can I have a look?" Kate asked. "There might be a different route we could take back."

While Kate studied the map, Helen took the opportunity to check her phone. She showed the phone to Kate and said, "There's no phone reception here, and it's nearly midday. I think it's best we return the way we came."

Looking up from the map, Kate said, "You're probably right." She threw back her head to call for the dogs, which had run on ahead, when she felt an arm across her back and a sharp, stabbing sensation in her shoulder.

# CHAPTER TWENTY-NINE

Mark Oates considered his options as he followed the two women at a safe distance. Excitement bubbled up as he realised where they were heading. This was going to be too easy. They were so intent on their conversation that they were oblivious to their surroundings. They might as well be walking along a busy high street for all the notice they were taking of the beautiful scenery around them. Typical of the younger generation. If it didn't have flashing lights and a pulsating soundtrack, it wasn't worth noticing.

It was increasingly unlikely he would have to go through the charade of helping them with a flat tyre. The dogs would be a minor inconvenience, but nothing he couldn't handle. He was good with dogs, and he'd never met a black Labrador with a nasty bone in its body. Disposing of them would add a little time, but he should still be able to get back to the car park and retrieve the car without any problems. Not that it mattered.

It was reassuring to know the car couldn't be traced back to him. His son had borrowed it from a friend without asking on his last visit. He'd developed an attachment to it while it had been safely stored inside a garage he had rented in Surrey. As it was the last direct link back to his son, he couldn't bear to leave it behind when he sold up. He'd moved it late one night to the new garage, where it had remained hidden ever since.

Snapping back to the present, Mark realised in another ten minutes, Kate and Helen would turn the corner and see the drop-down to a storage shed. It was where they stored the Christmas lights and Santa's sleigh and rarely visited the rest of the year. A sleigh pulled by real reindeer always drew the crowds. He briefly wondered where the reindeer were kept the other eleven months of the year. Deciding he didn't care, he looked to the sky and quietly thanked his wife, Betty. "You always said our National Trust membership would come in handy."

He remembered how often he'd walked the path with Betty holding hands, talking of the future, when they'd stayed in the area on weekend breaks. On one of those walks, they'd sheltered from a rainstorm in the storage hut. Without warning, the sky had turned dark and angry, blocking the summer sun. Initially, they'd pressed themselves against the wooden walls, keeping as far back as possible under the overhanging roof as the raindrops had thundered down around them. Lightning had streaked across the sky, and he'd noticed a glint in his peripheral vision. Reaching up, he'd felt along under the roof, and sure enough, there was a key hanging on a nail. The park obviously considered it unlikely someone would walk this way on the off chance of stealing a half-ton Santa's sleigh, so hadn't worried too much about security. After that, they'd made it a point to revisit the park at least once every three months. Hopefully, they hadn't moved the key since the last time he'd visited.

Mark pulled his cap lower over his face as he trudged on after the women. He rechecked his pockets. The feel of syringes buoyed his confidence. One in each pocket, ready for use. In a couple of minutes, they'd disappear around the corner. There he'd catch up to them. He'd manoeuvre himself to come between them. From there, it would be easy. Even if they turned at the last minute, what would they see? A harmless, middle-aged man enjoying a leisurely stroll through the woods. Just like they were.

It wouldn't be his first time. He was responsible for sticking the fatal needle in David as he blubbered over Betty when it was too late. Betty adored David, as only a mother can. He did everything in his power to keep the truth about their useless son from her. It would have broken her entirely. Seeing the disappointment on her face every time David cancelled his visits was painful enough. Each time, she'd dry her eyes and proudly tell everyone who would listen about her perfect son who worked so hard, even over the weekends. Only he knew how untrue that was.

Networking, David called it. Sipping Champagne with Richard to celebrate the stitching up another naïve fool, more like. Then, snorting whatever it was, he put up his nose. He behaved like Richard was his father. Richard this and Richard bloody that. It was all he could talk about. Sucking up to precious Richard and being at his beck and call day and night.

David soon came down to earth with a bump. When his drug and alcohol use grew out of control, Richard callously discarded him. Pretended, he hardly knew him. David moped about like a love-lost teenager. Too distraught to even visit when Betty was dying and asking for him every day. He didn't turn up until it was too bloody late. After all the pain he'd caused her, he had the nerve to sit at their kitchen table crying with snot bubbling from his nose.

The first time Mark had crossed the line and taken a life, it had been in a moment of passion. Madness, maybe. He wasn't sure if his display of grief at David's funeral had been genuine or the overwhelming sense of guilt at what he'd done. Either way, as the days and weeks passed, it slowly dawned on him that he'd gotten away with murder, and he knew he could do it again.

Mark looked up to see the time had arrived. He forced his clenched fists to relax and picked up the pace. Jittery with anticipation, he took deep breaths to calm himself. A bead of sweat trickled down his cheek. He wiped it away and pulled his cap down further. He shoved his hands into his jacket pockets to feel for the syringes.

# CHAPTER THIRTY

Simon flew down the steps to meet Detective Collins. "He's got my friend, Kate and Richard's daughter. They took the dogs for a walk this morning in the Valley Park, but they haven't returned." He held up his phone to the detective's face. "I've rung and rung, but they're not answering."

Detective Collins took a step back and sat on the bonnet of his car. The car dropped under his weight as he made himself comfortable. His bloodhound eyes looked Simon up and down. He held his arms up, palms facing Simon. "Now, calm down, lad. It's a beautiful day. Maybe your friends walked a little further than they intended."

Simon frantically waved his phone. "I can't get hold of them."

"Not surprising. The signal is intermittent at best out there. Why don't we go inside, and you can tell me what's been going on over a cup of tea?"

"You don't understand!" Simon shouted. "They weren't planning on being gone for long as they knew Alicia was probably going to be discharged from hospital. The hospital just rang. They can't get a hold of them."

"Their phones won't work any better than yours, son." Collins extended his arm towards the house. "You wanted to talk to me about a Mark Oates? Let's go inside and a have a cup of tea while you tell me all about him."

"Oh! For God's sake!" Simon said, heading towards the camper van. He didn't know which was worse, the man's patronising tone or his complete inability to grasp the urgency of the situation. Without appearing to move, Collins was in front of him, blocking his path. "Get out of my way," Simon said, trying to dodge past him. "You go and have a nice cup of tea if you like. I'm going to find my friend." A firm hand grabbed his arm and spun him around.

"Now, listen here, lad," Collins said, his heavy jowls wobbling. "I can see you're upset, but you can't go around accusing people without any proof. Not on my patch, anyway. I'm not going to allow you to turn up at this man's house and harass him. Yesterday, you were asking me to arrest a different young man, Ben Teobald. If needs be, I'll arrest you."

"Me! On what grounds?" Simon spluttered, trying to wriggle free.

"On the grounds, I believed you were going to carry out an assault."

Accepting he couldn't dislodge the brute, Simon stopped trying to twist out of the firm grip and said, "Let me go. I need to go to the Valley Park to find my friend. If it's not too late. He could be killing them right now."

"Who? Ben Teobald or Mark Oates? Is he now after your friend rather than Richard Fielding? Is that, right?" Collins scratched his head with his free hand, and said, "Now, why would he want to do that?"

"It's Helen, Richard's daughter he's after. But my friend is with her. Please, release me so I can find her before it's too late."

"I'll tell you what. My throat is parched, and I was looking forward to a cup of tea. How about you come with me, and I'll drive us both out to Valley Park. You can buy me a cup of tea in the café by the gift shop, and then we'll go looking for your friend. My son works there. He can take us around the park in his buggy. Be a damn sight quicker than walking. And on the way, you can coherently explain what on earth this is about. Deal?"

Simon sagged with relief. At last, he was getting somewhere with the buffoon. "Deal," he said, pulling away. Collins released his hold a fraction later, and Simon stumbled forward, nearly losing his footing. Realising he was on the driver's side, he turned to walk around the front of the car.

"Now, let's get started on the right footing," Fred said,

extending his hand. "I'm Fred. Detective Fred Collins."

Simon quickly shook the proffered damp hand. "I'm Simon. Can we get going?" He raced around to the passenger side and wrenched open the car door. Jumping in and slamming the door shut, he was surprised to see Fred already settled in the driver's seat.

"You'll treat my car with respect, or we're going nowhere," Fred said, sternly.

Biting down on his rising irritation and the urge to scream and shout, Simon mumbled, "Sorry. But can we please get going?"

Travelling through the lanes, Simon ran through everything he'd found out about Mark Oates. Once he'd completed his story, he glanced at the car's speedometer. "Can't you drive any faster? Don't you have a blue light to stick on the roof?"

Fred chuckled. "You've sure got an active imagination. There's no point us killing ourselves while your friend is having a stroll around the gift shop. Tell me, why would this Oates fellow have called an ambulance if he was so intent on killing Richard Fielding?"

Exasperated by the sedate speed of the car, Simon snapped, "I haven't worked out why he rang for an ambulance, but you haven't been listening to me. Helen is worried sick about her parents. She would have been constantly checking her phone. If there was no signal, she would have wanted to leave ages ago. The only thing that's moving at a leisurely pace is us."

Slowing the car's speed, Fred tapped a number on his phone set, attached to the console. Leaving it on the loudspeaker, he said, "Hi, Tom. It's your dad. I'll be at the park in a couple of minutes. I have a young man with me who thinks his friend is," turning to look at Simon, he carefully said, "lost in the park. Any chance you could meet us and take us around in a buggy to look for her?"

"No problem. I'll meet you by the entrance."

Fred drove through the park entrance and along a long winding driveway to the car park at a slow pace, sending Simon's blood pressure through the roof. He ground his teeth and scanned the surrounding area. Paths crisscrossed and branched off in all directions, up and down hills and through dense woodland. "We're going to need help. Three people can't possibly cover this much ground. It would take days," he said with a sinking heart.

Fred cruised into a car space and pulled out a park membership card from the glove compartment. Taking his time to position it squarely in the window, he shook his head at Simon, already outside the car, turning in wild circles. He heaved himself out of the car and checked and double-checked the car was locked. Leaning over the roof of the car, Fred said, "That's why we're going to start by checking the cars. There's no point us raising a hullabaloo if they're not even in the park. What's the make, model and registration number of the car?"

Simon panicked. He couldn't remember the registration number. "It's a green Mini with a white roof. It's this year's registration, but I can't remember all of it." Racking his brains, he added, "There's a golf-ball-shaped air freshener hanging from the rear-view mirror."

"That's a start. What colour are the seats?"

"White, I think."

"Ah! Here he is."

An ancient golf buggy came trundling across the car park. There was no mistaking it was driven by Fred's son. He could have been his twin brother, born thirty years later. Simon judged him to be in his late twenties, despite his already thinning hair. The same round face with a piggy nose and bloodhound eyes beamed at them as he approached. He stopped the buggy next to Simon and offered his pudgy hand. Having learnt from his father, there was no point trying to skip polite niceties, and despite the urgency, he shook the man's hand.

Simon desperately wanted to wipe his hand on his jeans after holding the clammy hand, but resisted and said, "Please. My friend has been missing for some time." With eyes darting around the park, he added, "Is there any chance of you arranging a full search party?"

Tom gave Simon a polite smile and turned to his father with a raised eyebrow.

"We're looking for a green mini with a white roof," Fred said.

A shadow of concern flicked across Tom's face. "What time did your friend arrive?" he asked Simon.

"Shortly after ten o'clock, I'd guess," Simon replied, watching a silent exchange between father and son. "Do you know something? Has something happened?"

"Maybe," Tom replied. "Hop on the back."

Simon jumped onto the bench seat at the rear of the golf buggy while Tom and his father climbed onto the two front seats. They sat shoulder to shoulder, their massive frames blocking his line of sight to the front. Simon silently seethed when Tom whispered in his father's ear before moving off. What was it they didn't want him to hear?

Unbearably slow minutes later, Alicia's Mini, surrounded by orange and white traffic cones, came into view. Tom drove as cautiously as his father, so Simon hopped off the side and jogged towards the car. Seeing the damage to the two rear tyres brought him up short. He interlocked his fingers behind his head and walked in small circles, desperately searching the horizon for an explanation. Hoping against hope, Kate would appear with a car mechanic, wondering what the fuss was about.

The buggy slowly came to a halt, and Fred clambered down at a laborious pace. He gradually lowered his substantial body to crouch next to one of the slashed tyres. He pulled a handkerchief from his pocket and mopped his brow as he inspected the damage. "When was the damage reported, son?"

"Just shy of eleven o'clock by a passer-by. We've no idea when the damage was done." Tom scratched the back of his head. "We expected the owners to make a complaint when they returned to their car. We planned on taking it from there and refunding their entrance fee."

"Very generous of the park," Fred said, without a hint of sarcasm.

"Now, will you take my concerns seriously and arrange a search of the park?" Simon said.

Fred used the side of the car to haul himself up. Ignoring Simon, he addressed Tom. "Have any falls or suspicious activity been reported, today?"

Tom tapped the walkie-talkie attached to the top of his belt. "Nothing out of the ordinary. A bunch of kids tearing around like hooligans, but nothing else."

"Contact the park manager to fill him in and say I want to talk to him as soon as possible. I'll call the station to see if there's anyone free who can help with the search."

"Aren't they still out looking for Sue Evans?" Tom asked.

Fred shook his head. "It turned out to be a false alarm. She was away visiting friends."

Simon kicked at the gravel surface, wondering if it was the same Sue Evans who Kate had met when she was out running. The conversation between Collins and his son had moved on when he interrupted them. "Was the supposed missing woman, Sue Evans from Leighterton?"

Both men turned to look at him with identical looks of annoyance at his interruption. Finally, Fred nodded, "Yes, it was."

"This is going to sound like a long shot, but could you ring her and ask if she saw Richard fall from his horse? I might know why Mark Oates called for an ambulance."

Fred gave an exaggerated sigh but pulled out his phone. He walked a short distance away to make the call. He returned a few minutes later, looking thoughtful. "You were right about her being there. She was in the adjacent field when she heard the commotion and ran to the gate. A grey-haired man was kneeling over Richard in the road. He refused her offer of help and said he was calling an ambulance."

# CHAPTER THIRTY-ONE

Knowing there would be no signal, Mark quickly closed the distance between himself and the two women as soon as he saw the phone in the girl's hand. He plunged the syringes simultaneously into their shoulders just as he'd practised. They wavered, then fell like dead weights either side of him. He looked down, feeling satisfied. Practice makes perfect.

The dogs continued sniffing the ground, unaware of what was happening behind them. They turned only when they heard the dull thud of the women hitting the ground. They came bounding back and ran in circles, occasionally pausing to lick the women's faces, thinking it was a game. Before they realised something was wrong, Mark pulled the dog leads from around Kate's neck and captured the two dogs.

Checking the area for other walkers, Mark decided to get the dogs inside the shed before they started to bark and attract attention. They followed him politely on their leads with their tails wagging. He felt along underneath the roof eaves and unhooked the key to the heavy padlock on the door. He patted the dogs before leaving them inside the shed. They started to whine, but that was better than them barking in the open.

He jogged up the bank and pulled first Kate, then Helen off the path to the top of the bank. To save energy, he rolled them down the bank. Momentum built, and gravity took over, depositing them by the shed entrance. Mark slithered down the bank after them. He picked up Kate from under her arms and dragged her inside the shed. After struggling to lift his son's dead weight upstairs, he'd joined a gym. In comparison, dragging Kate along the ground was easy. Returning for Helen, he noticed the flattened grass and drag marks with annoyance.

Inside the shed, he pulled the tape and rope from his inside pocket. Infuriated by the dogs getting in the way, he kicked and thumped them until they whelped and finally slunk away to watch him from the corner of the shed. He slipped the women's mobile phones and the car keys into his pocket before taping their mouths and tying their ankles together and their hands behind their backs.

He wasn't sure how long they would stay unconscious, and he needed to disguise the drag marks, lose the dogs, remove Simon from the picture and kill Richard. He was relieved neither of the women had seen him. Once Richard was dead, he wasn't concerned about whether they were found alive or not. In their case, he would leave the outcome to chance. When the elusive Sue Evans resurfaced, she wouldn't be so lucky. She had seen too much in the lane, and her fake concern annoyed him.

While running the busy schedule through his head, he spotted a pile of hessian sacks used by Santa to distribute presents to the children, thrown in the corner. They were perfect for his intended use. It was harder than he anticipated, but finally, he had both women in their own sack with the drawstring pulled tight at the top. He dragged them to the back of the shed behind the sleigh, then threw the large cardboard boxes covered in Christmas wrapping paper over the top of them.

Outside, he couldn't think of a way to un-trample the flattened grass. He grabbed a fallen branch and brushed away the drag marks on the gravel leading to the shed door. Cringing at the grass bank, he doubted himself for the first time. He should have stuck to the original plan of helping them with the car's flat tyres. They would start searching the area when the park closed, and the Mini was spotted. He had to hope even if they noticed the grass and looked inside the shed, they wouldn't find anything. He checked his pocket for his compass and returned inside, approaching the dogs with the slip leads. Although wary of him after their kicking, they obediently followed him outside. He headed to his right, dragging the dogs behind him. If he continued north in a straight line, he would come to the road between Leighterton and Bromley Heath.

Away from the maintained tracks, the terrain was uneven, and he tripped several times on exposed tree roots. On one occasion, he fell flat on his face, scratching his arm and bruising the side of his face. A couple of times, he was forced to detour from his intended route as the way was blocked with brambles. The fresh breeze forecasted didn't materialise, and the temperature rose. His skin prickled in the heat as it became slick with sweat. He could smell the stench of his own stale sweat as he marched onwards, dragging the reluctant dogs. He fought the urge to abandon his coat which became heavier with every step. At least it protected his upper body from the stinging nettles and thistles. His legs had been stung to the point they'd gone from painful, through hot pulsing to numb.

Finally, he heard the drone of passing cars, which strengthened his resolve to keep forging ahead when he felt like giving up. The roadside hedgerow came into sight on the far side of a field of oilseed rape. He made his way around the edge of the field on a narrow verge of grass, brambles and nettles. Negotiating the thin band of tangled weeds was made increasingly difficult with the dogs constantly looking back for the girls. He gritted his teeth and roughly dragged them on. He had to get them to the other side of the main road so they wouldn't lead the search party directly back to the shed.

The metal gate that led out onto the road was padlocked. He tied one dog to the gate, waited for a lull in the traffic, lifted the other over and then repeated the exercise. He crossed over the road and was relieved to see a public footpath sign. He led the dogs through the kissing gate and removed their collars and leads. He threw a stick, and as the dogs chased after it, he slipped back through the gate, closing it behind him. Even if the dogs were microchipped by the time some do-gooder found and took them to their local vets to check for ownership, it would be too late.

He had planned to return to the park car park the way he'd come. Pulling strings of sticky grass, burrs and brambles from his jacket, he changed his mind. It would take longer, but he'd follow the road around the perimeter, instead. In the blazing sun, he realised he stood out wearing a heavy jacket. He wriggled out of it and carried it over his arm until he came to a road sign. He removed his keys and wallet from the pockets, neatly folded the jacket and pushed it under the adjacent hedge to collect later. He marched on, not intending to slow to a stroll until he reached the park entrance.

He was convinced Kate was the brighter of the nosey duo. She'd been far more alert when they'd visited. Asking the harder questions and examining the photograph of Betty and David. Simon had been too smug about his knowledge of old bread ovens to pay much attention.

Mark had to assume they had discussed the Facebook account, but he doubted Simon could work out much more by himself, and he was confident nothing could be traced back to him. If he was lucky, the women wouldn't be reported missing until early evening. Late afternoon at the earliest. The boy was physically stronger, but he had the element of surprise and spare syringes tucked away in his car's glove compartment.

Mark slowed his walking as he entered the main gates to the park and followed the twisty drive that led to the car park. He broke out in a cold sweat when he was forced to jump to the side to allow four marked police cars with lights blazing and sirens wailing to pass him. His heart raced. He stood still, looking about him, deciding what to do. Turn around and walk away? Keep going? He took deep breaths to calm himself. Dithering in the middle of the road would draw attention to himself. As would rushing away. The police cars had taken no notice of him. Why should they? He was a fully paid-up member of the National Trust, making use of his membership on a beautiful sunny day.

He willed one foot in front of the other and walked on, his car keys already in his hand. The emergency was probably nothing to do with him. Anything could have happened. A pensioner having a heart attack in the heat. An unruly child falling from a tree. A pregnant woman going into labour. It was likely the local police had very little reason to tear through the lanes and probably jumped at every opportunity when it presented itself. He mopped his face dry with his damp handkerchief and nearly convinced himself all was well until he entered the car park and saw uniformed police officers milling around the Mini.

Giving them a cursory glance, he looked down and hurried to his car which was parked several rows behind. He was a matter of feet away from his car when he heard someone approaching from his right.

"Do you have any idea what is going on?"

Mark looked up into the anxious eyes of a mother pushing a double pushchair. A baby was asleep on one side. On the other, a hot and fractious toddler kicked and squirmed against the harness holding her in place.

"No idea, I'm afraid," Mark said, before quickly turning away.

A deep voice from behind him said, "A car has been vandalised. They're trying to find the owner, who they believe is in the park somewhere. They're asking for volunteers to help with a search and asking everyone leaving whether they've seen them."

Mark turned, to find himself nearly toe-to-toe with a tall, rugged-looking man. Stepping back, he muttered, "Oh dear. What is the world coming to?"

"I know. I'm going to volunteer. The more feet on the ground, the quicker they'll find the two women."

Mark swallowed. "How do they know it's two women?"

"Good point. Dunno," the man said, scratching his belly. "Could be from the car registration? Are you coming to find out? I'm sure they'll appreciate the help. Community spirit and all that."

"Well … umm … Sorry. My wife is waiting for me at home. She's not well and frets terribly if I'm late."

"Fair enough," the man replied.

Mark slid into his car seat as a quivering wreck. He had to pull himself together in case he was asked questions at the exit. His hands shook as he gripped the steering wheel, and his rubbery legs didn't have the power to push down on the pedals. His mind raced as he sat motionless, staring out the front windscreen. He screamed when he heard a tap on the window. Recovering himself, he lowered the window. "Can I help you?"

A middle-aged woman peered at him. "You've been sat there a while, and I thought I'd better check on you. Are you feeling okay? You look awfully pale. You're not having a heart attack or a stroke, are you? Can you raise your right arm?"

"Yes. No. I'm perfectly fine. I think maybe the heat got to me, but I'm feeling better now."

The woman looked dubious but stepped back from the car, and said, "If you're sure?"

"I am. Thank you for your concern," Mark replied, before raising the window and starting the car. He took a deep breath and pulled away. Annoyed with himself and his moment of weakness, he resolved to do better in future.

He told the constable at the gate he hadn't seen anything amiss and retrieved his jacket without incident. His heart rate gradually slowed as he drove along. No one suspected him of anything, but he was done with the elaborate plans which allowed too many chances for failure. He checked the glove compartment for his supply of syringes and the serrated hunting knife. He'd head directly to Clenchers Mill, kill the stupid boy and lie in wait for Alicia and Richard to return from the hospital. This time, he'd make damn sure they wouldn't survive.

# CHAPTER THIRTY-TWO

Simon knew his inability to sit still was annoying the hell out of everyone, but he couldn't help it. Sick with guilt and apprehension, he got up from the plastic seat in the park manager's office and paced to the window. Things were happening all around him, but not fast enough. His brain used every agonising moment to create increasingly gruesome scenarios of what Mark was doing to Kate and Helen. Each fuelled his self-reproach and sense of helplessness. His tense muscles screamed for an outlet.

His skin prickled, and a bead of sweat ran down his side. He struggled to breathe air into his lungs in the tiny airless room. Overheated, trapped and breathless, he shot out of the door. He stood outside, desperately searching the forest tracks, gulping in mouthfuls of fresh air until his lungs ached. He bent forward with his hands on his knees, praying Kate would walk out of the woods unscathed. The pressure of a large hand on his back agitated rather than calmed him.

"Take slow, deep breaths, son. It will pass," Fred said, rubbing Simon's back.

Between ragged breaths and clenched teeth, Simon replied, "Where the hell are they?"

"All the park rangers are on the lookout for them. They're checking the paths and the various sheds dotted around." Looking into the distance, Fred added, "If they're out there, they'll be found."

"What if they're already dead? What if he snatched them and

has taken them elsewhere?"

"I've double-checked. He would need a vehicle to transport them, and there is only one route a vehicle could take in and out of the park."

Simon pushed himself upright, his mind racing in time with his heart. "You're kidding, right?" Agitated, he paced in small circles, his fists clenched. "There must be numerous gates and other exits from the park. What if he parked by an external fence and enticed them over in some way? Kate would have trusted him. She even liked Mark." Bowing his head and covering his face with his hands, he moaned, "I didn't make the connection until after they left for the park." He looked at Fred with pleading eyes. "Why didn't I make the connection sooner?"

"You need to calm yourself, son. We don't know for sure anyone has snatched your friends. They could have lost track of time or become lost. One of them may have done something as simple as tripping and twisting an ankle. That would slow them down."

Simon furiously shook his head. Anger and frustration scorched through his veins. "Why won't you listen to me? They were waiting for a call from the hospital. They wouldn't have gone that far. If one of them had fallen like you suggest, they would have used their phones to call for help. Something bad has happened to them. And it's all my fault."

"Reception is patchy in places." Fred gave a heavy sigh, before saying, "An unknown vehicle on the paths or driving through the open spaces and farmland would have been reported." He lay his hand on Simon's shoulder while he retrieved his ringing phone from his shirt pocket. After thanking the caller, Fred said, "All the park vehicles have been accounted for. If there's an abductor out there, he's on foot."

Simon's eyes searched Fred's face, wanting to believe him. Despite his previous misgivings about the man, he had quickly taken charge and thought on his feet. The photo of Kate from his phone had been scanned, and all the searchers had a copy. Officers had been dispatched to the hospital to update Alicia and Richard and obtain a picture of Helen. While he'd been pointlessly shouting and pacing, Fred had been asking all the right questions. In comparison, Simon felt he was next to useless.

In the distance came the sound of approaching sirens. Fred said, "Everyone available is coming to search for your friends. I have been listening to you, and I'm going to head out to speak to Mark Oates."

"Can I come with you? Please."

"It's highly irregular, but why not? If you're sure you wouldn't prefer to wait here for news about your friend?"

Simon caught sight of the flashing blue lights nearing the park entrance. He was torn. He wanted to be here for when they found Kate and Helen, but he was positive that Mark would know where they were. Even if the unthinkable had happened. Fred had done all the right things here, but only after the slashed tyres had been discovered. Had he done enough to completely convince him that Mark was a dangerous man and behind it all? Because, if Fred didn't believe that without any doubts, he wouldn't push hard enough for answers.

"Well, son? What do you want to do?"

Simon managed a small smile. "Will you promise to drive a little faster?"

Fred gruffly replied, "There's no need to go breaking our necks. There's a speed limit for a reason," and turned to walk away.

Simon jogged a few paces to catch up with Fred. Fred's seemingly casual pace covered the ground deceptively fast. "I'm coming with you if that's okay?"

In the stuffy confines of the car, Simon clenched his fists and bit his tongue the entire journey to stop himself from urging Fred to put his foot down. He guessed part of the reason he was in the car was that Fred wanted to keep him out of the way of the search party. He needed to calm his racing mind to be of any use to anyone. He tensed and reached for the door handle when the row of cottages came into sight.

While Fred parallel parked a short distance away from Mark's cottage, secured the vehicle, and carefully folded the wing mirror in, Simon leapt from the car and ran to the front door. He hadn't taken much notice when Mark had turned up at Clenchers Mill, but he was sure the small blue car parked outside was the one he'd been driving that day. Simon repeatedly banged on the door and shouted through the letterbox. Fred strolled up behind him with his phone in his hand. "I've run the plates." Indicating the blue car behind them, he said, "That's his car, so I assume he can't be far away."

"Well, he's not answering the door!" Simon shouted back.

Fred calmly asked, "Is there a rear entrance? He might be relaxing in the back garden, out of earshot."

Simon thought back to the day they sat on the patio discussing Richard's accident when they thought Mark was the hero who called the ambulance. It hadn't even crossed his mind, he did so only because the woman in the adjacent field had seen him. Through stupid jealousy, he had been too busy trying to pin the attacks on Ben to question Mark's version of events. Fred was right. He had to start thinking with a cool head.

Fighting to control his emotions and clear his head left a vacuum for thoughts about his sister's death to enter. Up popped the question he always asked himself. In the hell of the arena, after the explosion, did anyone hold his sister's hand to comfort her in the moments before her death? He banged on Mark's front door, blinking away the tears threatening to fall from his eyes. He couldn't let anything happen to Kate and be responsible for another death. He just couldn't.

"Well? Is there a rear entrance?" Fred asked, a tinge of impatience in his voice.

"Umm, I think there is a small gate at the bottom of his garden. Where it leads. I have no idea."

Simon turned away from the door to see Fred knocking on the next-door house. A tall, erect man with an amazing moustache answered the door. It was thick and bushy, with the ends teased into a tight curl. The owner pulled back his lips, giving them both an eerie smile that revealed crooked, yellow teeth. "Can I help you, gentlemen?"

Fred fished in his pockets, checking one, then another. The neighbour watched him quizzically until Fred finally located the correct pocket and pulled out his warrant card. "We're interested in speaking to your neighbour, Mark Oates. His car is parked outside, but he isn't answering the door. We wondered if he was in his back garden and unable to hear us?"

Glancing at the car, the gentleman, shrugged. "He could be walking that yappy little dog of his." He stopped and twirled the end of his moustache with his finger and thumb. "Only, I thought I heard it barking a while ago."

"Is there a way we can get to the back of the house?" Fred asked.

The gentleman stepped out of his house, onto the narrow pavement. He pointed along the road, and said, "Walk four houses down, and you'll see a sign for a footpath. It runs along the back of all these houses. You'll be able to see over the gate to check whether he's in his back garden."

Fred slipped his warrant card into his back trouser pocket. Simon made a mental note of where it was to save time should he need to show it again. Fred said, "Thank you, very much, Mr. ...?"

"Sam. Sam Ross." He stepped back into his doorway and tilted his head. "I'm pleased I could be of some assistance."

By the time Sam had closed his door, Simon was on the footpath. He jogged along, counting the houses as he went. Stopping outside the low metal gate to Mark's garden, he recognised it immediately. The gate swung open. If it hadn't, even Fred would have been able to step over it with ease. Simon raced through the terraced garden. The dog inside the house barked and scratched at the bottom of the patio doors. Simon yanked the handle. Firmly locked, it didn't budge.

Fred appeared behind Simon. "It's unusual for people around here to keep their back doors locked if they're in. Especially on a beautiful day like this."

"Where is he? His car is out the front, and he isn't walking his dog." The dog continued to bark as Simon marched along the back wall of the house until he came to a wooden door in need of a lick of paint. The old black handle turned smoothly in his hand. The door creaked open on rusty hinges, revealing nothing more than a wood store. He quickly returned to Fred. "Can we break a window to get in?"

Fred hoisted up his trousers, a useless exercise as they immediately rolled back under his flabby stomach. "Now, hold your horses, lad." His forehead creased as he looked the house up and down. He cocked his head to one side to listen to the dog barking. "That dog is starting to sound hoarse, don't you think? It could be, he's in desperate need of water."

Simon's eyes ran along the upper floors, noting all the upstairs windows were closed. "We've got to do something."

Fred mopped his forehead and said, "I feel there may be reasonable grounds for us to have concerns for the wellbeing of this householder and the wee dog inside."

Simon said, "Great. I'll find a stone."

Fred caught his arm. "I don't think criminal damage by a member of the public is called for." He pulled out a jumble of thin metal sticks from a front pocket. He hitched his trousers up again and crouched by the patio doors. He squinted at the lock, before saying, "I'll have this open in a jiffy."

Not wanting to hover and get an eyeful of Fred's builder's bum, Simon headed across to the patio table and chairs. He'd taken a couple of steps when he heard the unmistakable sound of the whoosh of the door being slid open. "How did you …?" he started to ask, but Fred had already disappeared inside.

The dog shot out past Simon into the garden to relieve itself. Inside was neat and tidy, precisely as Simon remembered it. Fred was busy poking about in kitchen cupboards. Simon went directly to the side cabinet in the living room and picked up the framed photograph that had caught Kate's eye on their previous visit.

There was nothing remarkable about the smiling family picture. He scrutinised it carefully before turning it over. The backing bulged, suggesting there was something behind the picture. He folded back the metal clips that held the frame together and removed the back. Behind it, he found a picture of David Oates and Richard Fielding sipping from champagne flutes on an expensive-looking yacht. Their shorts and T-shirts, tan and cloudless blue sky suggested they were nowhere near the grey skies of Skegness. Turning the picture over, he read the inscription. 'To my almost son, July 10th, 2017.' Simon kept hold of the photograph but clipped the frame back together. Replacing the family photograph on the cabinet, he pulled out the lower drawers. In the first drawer he tried, he found the funeral service sheet for Mrs. Elizabeth Oates. The funeral took place on July 10th, 2017. No wonder Mark was so disappointed with his son.

"Find anything?" Fred called from the kitchen.

Simon showed him the photograph and funeral service, noticing when he handed them over, unlike him, Fred was wearing blue plastic gloves.

Fred examined the two items before handing Simon a pair of matching gloves. "Here, put these on. The occupant could be upstairs in urgent need of our assistance. We'd better go and check."

The wooden staircase led them to a small landing with three closed doors. A family bathroom and two large bedrooms. All were spotlessly clean. One bedroom had flowery wallpaper and smelt of lavender air freshener and washing detergent. The other, while also neat with freshly laundered sheets, had the air of recent occupancy. Fred checked the wardrobe and chest of drawers while Simon backed out of the room and took the narrow staircase leading to a third floor, built into the attic.

The attic room was unbearably hot and stuffy due to the sun blazing down through the dormer window and the heat generated by a rank of laptops lining two of the walls. One computer screen showed a continuous flow of coded letters and numbers. The remaining screens were blank. Simon checked each in turn, but they were all password-protected.

Fred entered the room, complaining of the heat. He whistled at the hum of the computers. "Find anything useful on them?"

Simon slumped back in the computer chair. "I can't get into any of them. We need to take these to someone who can get past the passwords."

"'I'm afraid we can't do that. Other than the fact the son appeared to have chosen a cruise over attending his mother's funeral, there's no physical evidence that Mark Oates has done anything wrong."

"You've seen how meticulously neat he is. He wouldn't leave things hanging around or stuffed into drawers. Any evidence will be stored on these computers."

"Sorry, son. There's nothing here that warrants seizing them. I had a genuine reason for entering the house to check if he was okay because of the barking dog. We're going to have to leave everything as we found it."

"Even the photograph and funeral service?"

"I might fail to notice they haven't been put back in their proper place. Now, come along. We need to leave. I promise I'll interview him the moment he reappears. I can ask him to voluntarily allow access to his computer records."

Simon gave a hollow laugh. "Like that's going to happen. He'll wipe everything clean before handing them over if he does at all."

"Without any proof of wrongdoing, I can't force the issue."

Before returning to the car, Fred knocked on the next-door house. "Sorry to bother you again. Mark Oates doesn't appear to be in, although the dog is. Have you any idea where he might be, considering his car is parked outside. Someone in the village he's friendly with, maybe?"

"No idea. He keeps himself to himself, mostly. Same as we do," Sam replied, stroking his moustache.

Tilting his head towards the blue car, Fred asked, "And that's the only car he drives?"

The neighbour leaned forward and spoke in a conspiratorial voice. "Well! I haven't seen him in another vehicle, but he does rent one of the garages over there," he said, pointing to a row of low stone buildings set back from the lane on the corner. "The farmer up the road rents them out. We were hoping to take one on after the previous occupants left, but it appears a sneaky deal was done, and possession of the garage was passed to Mark. Very annoying and unfair as he doesn't use it and continues to park his car here. My partner is forced to park his car at the end of the village."

"Do you happen to know which garage is his?"

"I do. It's the second one from the left."

Fred and Simon walked to the small block of garages. They were old stone stables, adapted to their new purpose with roll-up metal shutters fitted at the front. Simon grasped the handle of the second shutter and was surprised to find it unlocked. He pulled the shutter up sufficiently high for them both to duck inside. The garage was empty, but there was an oil stain on the concrete floor. Simon pressed his fingers into the stain. Showing the brown tips of his fingers to Fred, he said, "It's fresh."

Fred pulled out his phone. "I'll check to see if any other vehicles are registered to him. Or possibly his deceased wife."

"Try the son as well, David Oates," Simon suggested.

Nodding his head, Fred said, "Meanwhile, do you want a lift back to the park or to Clenchers Mill?"

While Simon was keen to return to the park, he also wanted the freedom of his own transport. "Clenchers Mill, please. I'll go and wait in the car."

Fred threw him the car keys while he patiently waited for someone on the other end of his phone to answer his queries.

# CHAPTER THIRTY-THREE

Once he'd put a fair distance between himself and the park, unfortunately in the opposite direction to Clenchers Mill, Mark pulled over into a lay-by. His breathing and heart rate had returned to normal, and he congratulated himself on how well he'd handled things, despite the forced change of plans. Nobody of any relevance had seen him enter or leave the park, and he would be driving towards Clenchers Mill from a completely different direction.

He doubted the two people who'd spoken to him in the car park could describe him in any detail. There was no reason they should suspect him of any involvement in the missing women. The brief conversation probably wouldn't have even registered next to their excitement about being involved in a police drama. The only benefit of him being an utterly unremarkable man who had led a perfectly average life. Never one to rock the boat or stand up and make a fuss. So nondescript that he rapidly faded into the background. A skill that improved with age. The invisibility cloak, so coveted by the young Harry Potter generation was the unwanted mantle of the elderly. At best, his life amounted to no more than a footnote in the wider scale of things.

Small and insignificant. That's how David saw him next to the charming, charismatic, perfect, bloody Richard Fielding. Mark's anger returned when he thought of David sipping champagne in the Mediterranean, when he should have been at Betty's funeral. He wasn't a religious man, but he hoped to God she hadn't been looking down on them that day, searching the small congregation for her wonderful, dutiful son. He thumped the steering wheel, cursing. He should have bloody been there. Not with that oily snake charmer.

Claiming ownership of my son. The barefaced cheek of the creepy, little man. Promised our David, the Earth, I expect. For what? To dump him a few months later. He even left his poor wife when a younger, more attractive model came along.

Bristling with renewed indignation, Mark started the car. He'd show them a thing or two. There was life in the old dog yet.

Torn between keeping his presence unknown and making a quick getaway, he left his car a short distance away, along the old byway that ran parallel to the rear of the Clencher Mill's grounds. Clambering out of the air-conditioned interior, he was hit by the humid, warm air. His stiff limbs were painful and reluctant to move. He'd forgotten how taxing the terrain he'd crossed with the dogs had been. Once this was all over, he'd treat himself to a stay in one of those posh spa hotels. He'd promised Betty they would go one day. Only her health deteriorated quicker than expected. When they were due to go, she said she'd wanted to stay home in case David came. Grinding his teeth, Mark ignored his complaining muscles, climbed the fence and marched towards the rear of Clenchers Mill.

He slowed his pace before crossing the paddock closest to the house. Three horses raised their heads and eyed him suspiciously as he moved around the edge of the field, keeping close to the tree line. He slipped through the gate and dashed to the rear of the stable block. He edged around the side, watching the house. There was no sign of movement, and from his vantage point, he couldn't tell whether there were any cars on the front drive. He crept along the back of the stables to view the holiday cottages on the other side.

Taking a deep breath, he broke cover and walked the short distance to the cottage, checking the syringe in his pocket all the while. After knocking on the front and rear doors and peering in the windows, he accepted Simon was not inside.

He walked back to the stable block and crouched down to think. Gone where? To join the search at the park? To collect Richard and Alicia from the hospital? Gone, gone? Or was he in the main house?

It was so much easier moving around under cover of darkness. Did he have the patience to wait until it became dark? The women would remain unconscious for a few hours. Even if they came around prematurely, they'd be disorientated. With their hands and feet bound and a rope tightly wound around the tops of the sacks, they wouldn't be able to move far. Their mouths were taped so they couldn't call for help. Worst case scenario, if they were found, neither had seen him. Nobody would come looking for him. Still, he didn't want to stay here until he got cramps in his legs. Strike when the iron's hot. That's what his mother used to say.

He checked his pockets to feel the three syringes and his folding hunting knife were safely in place. He pushed himself upright and moved along the rear of the stable block. Crouching low, he ran along the length of the stone wall, which would bring him out closer to the rear garden of the main house. Dashing from ornamental bush to ornamental bush, he zigzagged his way to the rear of the house, silently thanking the landscape gardener for making it so easy. He crept onto the patio, keeping a watchful eye for any movement within the silent house. Nothing moved, and there were no muffled sounds from a television or radio playing in the background. He stepped up to peer through a window when the sound of an approaching vehicle set his heart racing.

There were plenty of places to lay undetected in the garden, but then he wouldn't know what was going on at the front of the house. He pulled the knife from his pocket, and grasping it tightly in front of him, he eased his way around the side of the house as the sound of gravel crunching under tyres grew louder. He crawled past the massive picture window and inched his way to the corner of the house. He pressed his body tight against the wall as a car door opened and slammed shut.

"I'll grab something of Kate's and Helen's and be back in five minutes."

The shrill sound of a phone ringing and the car door re-opening, was followed by a voice Mark didn't recognise. "I need to go straight back. The dog handlers are going to be delayed for another one to two hours."

Mark pressed his forehead to the wall. Think. Think. Simon is returning to the house, alone. You could catch him by surprise. Leave him for dead in the cottage. But how would that help? The alarm would be raised, and the house would be swarming with people. It was Richard and Alicia he wanted. Everyone else was collateral damage.

The second voice, presumably a police officer, continued, "Why don't you wait for Richard and Alicia to arrive back here? You could give the girl's clothes to the officer who drops them off and talk to Richard about Mark Oates's son. There might be some little snippet that he didn't think to mention when he was questioned in the hospital. Something that'll help us understand how Mark thinks or the places he goes."

"I hadn't thought about it. I'm not sure Richard had even met the rest of the family." After a short consideration, Simon asked, "They will be safe here, won't they?"

"I'm not happy about them staying here. I'd feel much better if they booked themselves into a hotel for the night as I suggested, but they'll be returning with another two officers. One to watch the front of the house and one the rear. It's the best I could do."

"At least you convinced them they'd be more of a hindrance than a help with the search if they went straight to the park."

"There is that. Although what help he thought he could be with a broken leg is beyond me. See what you can find out from him, and I'll see you in a bit."

The brief exchange that told Mark all he needed to know about what was going on was followed by crunching gravel as the car slowly turned. The sound diminished as the car drove out along the drive. Next, he heard a key turning in a lock and a door opening but not closing.

Mark turned around keeping his back close to the side of the house, listening for movement. His annoyance they were on to him was tempered by the opportunity they'd handed him on a plate. Had he ever thought he'd be heading off into the sunset, blissfully happy he'd achieved his aims without anyone realising it was him? Probably not. In any event, without Betty, was his life worth living?

He blocked the morbid thoughts from his mind. They would only send him spiralling back into depression. Revenge was the only thing that kept him going. A grin spread across his face. He should look on the bright side. It won't be a great deal of help having two local plods outside if I'm already inside.

# CHAPTER THIRTY-FOUR

Simon dashed up the stairs and grabbed Kate's running clothes which were screwed up in a ball in the middle of her room. Helen's room was neat and tidy and lacking in recently discarded clothes. Great, he thought. The only teenage girl that doesn't leave dirty clothes strewn across the floor. He assumed there must be a laundry basket somewhere, but he had no idea where. He opened a wardrobe door and peered inside. He pushed the hangers aside and checked the floor. He could only see clean, neatly ironed clothes, and they probably wouldn't have enough scent for the dogs. Feeling uncomfortable about invading her space, he checked the bed for nightwear. There, under the pillow, were pyjamas neatly folded. A quick sniff told him they'd been worn at least once.

Mark crept along the side of the house, listening to the car engine fading into the distance. As he had hoped when Simon had dashed inside the house, the front door hadn't clicked closed behind him. Listening to the sound of Simon moving around upstairs, he slipped through the open door and into the airy entrance hall. Not knowing how long it would be until Simon descended the stairs, he quickly crossed the room to stand in the far corner by the base of the staircase. He strained his ears to listen to what was happening upstairs.

Mark hoped that if Simon was going to wait for Richard and

Alicia to return, he might take a shower to pass the time. That would give him plenty of time to move through the house to find a temporary hiding place. Chuckling to himself, he thought, preferably one from where I can listen to this enlightening chat about me and the places I like to visit. He doubted he was ever David's topic of conversation when he was trailing after his idol, Richard. Instead of taking a shower, Simon appeared to be walking around the landing, looking inside rooms.

The footsteps became louder overhead, suggesting Simon was going to come back down the stairs, and he still hadn't found anywhere to hide. There was always the chance he wouldn't look back at the staircase and see him, but it was a major risk. Mark's heart was pounding, and he broke out in a sweat. Desperately looking around for something to hide behind, he spotted a door fitted into the base of the staircase. He hadn't seen it before as it was designed to blend in and only be noticeable on close inspection. Hearing Simon start to descend the stairs, he quietly pulled open the door and slipped inside the cupboard.

Before closing the door and plunging himself into darkness, Mark noted how large an area it was, filling most of the space under the substantial staircase. The front section was used for hanging coats and storing outside shoes and wellingtons. To his right, the ceiling gently tapered to the floor, following the contours of the staircase. Suitcases of various colours and sizes were stacked in the corner.

Mark edged his way past the coats and crawled along the floor until he reached the suitcases. Even if Simon entered the cupboard and pulled a coat from one of the hooks, he'd only see him if he looked directly in his direction. He dared not move to the back of the cupboard in case he knocked the suitcases over. He found a comfortable place to sit and wait, cradling the knife in his lap, just in case. He held his breath, listening to Simon cross the hallway. There was no sound of the front door opening and closing. Somewhere to his left, he heard the click of an internal door opening, so he assumed Simon was waiting downstairs for Richard and Alicia to return. Too bad he wouldn't be able to overhear their conversation from where he was.

Sitting in the dark, it occurred to Mark that the police escorting Richard and Alicia home would probably search the house, before taking up their surveillance positions outside. Considering the size of the house, he doubted it would be a thorough search, but it might be enough to discover him hiding in the most obvious place, the cupboard under the stairs. They would probably step into the cupboard and, at the very least run a torch along the back wall. While Simon was elsewhere in the house, he could take the risk of toppling one of the suitcases over to crawl behind them. If they looked undisturbed, he doubted the police would go to the trouble of pulling them all out to inspect the back of the cupboard. Not when there were countless rooms upstairs that needed checking.

In the dark, he cautiously lifted the suitcases one by one out of the way, listening all the time for the arrival of Richard and Alicia. He half-crawled, half-slid himself into the cramped space he'd made. Headspace was limited, forcing him to keep his head bent forward. He shuffled around to pull the displaced suitcases back around him, so he was completely hidden from sight.

Simon entered the kitchen and paced, checking the window on every lap for the car carrying Richard and Alicia to arrive. Having something to do, even something as menial as collecting clothes, helped him to keep a lid on his overwhelming fears. Waiting stretched his nerves to breaking point. Kate had to be found safe and well. She had to. He couldn't return to where he was before, knowing everything was his fault.

Kate had no idea what she meant to him. He teased her and joked around while keeping his true feelings to himself. Unwilling to burden her with the truth. No one should be expected to carry that sort of burden for someone else.

Before she careered into his life, he'd had everything planned. Maybe not in precise detail, but the overall picture was there to be coloured in. He had rented out the family house and land that his parents loved so much. After meeting the tenants, his guilt levels had surged as he'd suspected it wouldn't work out long term. He solved that problem by paying a land agent handsomely to deal with the fallout.

For himself, he'd planned a crazy summer in Europe. On the surface, he would appear to be living life to the full, taking on every challenge and making the most of his inheritance. People would disapprove of his apparent callous disregard of his family's fate, but no one would be worried about him or what his intentions might be. As far as anyone was concerned, he was just out for a good time, spending his late parent's money. The more dangerous and daring the adventures, the better.

When the summer sun faded, and the holidaymakers went home tired and sunburnt, he'd head for the Alps, laden down with the most ridiculously expensive malt whiskey he could lay his hands on. Book an expensive chalet and wait until the first blizzard warning. Head up as far as he could with the whiskey in a backpack and drink himself into oblivion. Warm from the alcohol, he'd throw off his outer clothes and lie down to sleep. Hypothermia would take over. The snow would cover him so no poor sod would have to find his frozen body, ever. What a wonderful way to go!

Then Kate had appeared needing his help, and his plans had been put on hold. He'd decided to stick around just long enough to put the crazy chick back on track. His last act on earth would be putting this confused, broken girl back together. One amazing, good deed before he shuffled his way from the unbearable act of living.

He stopped pacing to look out the window. Was that true? At first, all he'd wanted to do was sleep with her before they went their separate ways. But then something had happened. Hell, he even started believing in his stupid idea of becoming a private investigator and making his life bearable by helping others. After all, he didn't care what happened to him. It didn't matter if he put himself into dangerous situations. He'd planned on ending it all anyway. Only, it was Kate he'd put at risk, not himself. The façade came tumbling down. His wanton disregard for his own safety had threatened hers.

The walls of Alicia's kitchen closed in on Simon, making it hard to breathe. The chance of a full-blown panic attack increased with every second he remained in the house. He glanced out the window at the empty driveway. He couldn't stay in the airless room. He needed to be outside doing something. Anything to get Kate back. He scribbled a note for Alicia and Richard, grabbed the items of clothing he'd so carefully bagged and headed for the front door.

◆ ◆ ◆

Simon parked the camper van in the near-empty car park and hurried to the park manager's office. Inside, Fred was huddled with several other officers having an animated conversation while pointing to a map on the wall. Two tired-looking park rangers sat slumped in chairs listening to their conversation. Simon coughed loudly to catch their attention.

Turning, Fred said, "Good, you're back. The dogs have arrived earlier than expected, and there's been a development. Have you brought the items of clothing?"

Simon held up the two bags containing the clothes. "Yes, I've got them here." Placing the bags on the central table, he asked, "What development?"

"Your dogs have been found about two miles outside the park. They weren't wearing collars. The person who found them held onto them for a short while, asking around locally if anyone was missing two dogs. Only when he couldn't locate an owner did he think to take them to the nearest vet. Luckily, it was one of the vets we'd already contacted, and they were already on the lookout for two lost black Labradors."

"Where were they found?" Simon asked.

Fred waved him over to the map and pointed out the name of a village Simon didn't recognise, called Bromley Heath. Fred ran his finger across the map lower down. "This is the periphery of the park." Moving his finger from there to the village, he said, "The distance from here to where they were found is about two miles. If they came out of the park anywhere along here," he said, running his finger along the map. "They would have had to cross a busy, major road. Are they in the habit of running off, and would they have sufficient road sense to cross between an almost continuous stream of fast-moving traffic?"

Squinting at the map in the hope it would magically tell him where Kate was, Simon shook his head. "They might chase a rabbit or a deer for a short distance, but they would never stray that far from Kate. Certainly not out of sight. Albert, that's the smaller of the two, is petrified of traffic. He would only cross a fast road with cars whizzing by on his own, as a last resort."

Fred looked back at the officers, rubbing his chin. "So, how do we call it? Continue the search here or move on to where the dogs were found?"

Before any of the officers could respond, Simon said, "My dogs love Kate. They would not have left her of their own accord. Especially if they thought she was in danger or being threatened in some way."

"So, we take the dogs over to Bromley Heath and start searching where the dogs were picked up," one officer said.

Fred put his hands on his generous hips and looked the map up and down. "What if he grabbed them all in the park? He could have thrown the dogs from the car later to confuse the issue?"

"Then there's no point looking anywhere around here," the earlier officer said.

One of the rangers stood up, shaking his head. "You're trying to say an unauthorised vehicle drove across the park with two screaming women and two barking dogs without anyone noticing? Impossible."

Fred rotated his hips and stood up straight. "One set of dogs searches the park following Miss Chapman's scent. The other set goes out to Bromley Heath, to follow Miss Fielding's scent." Turning to Simon, he said, "Tell us which clothing is which, and then you need to go and collect your dogs before they end up in a shelter." As Simon started to object, Fred said, "I'll keep you updated. You can return to help with the search after you've sorted your dogs. I promised the vets you'd be straight over to collect them."

Everyone filed out of the office together. The dog handlers to prepare their dogs for the search, and Simon to collect Alfred and Albert. A few steps outside the door, Simon stopped and turned, causing a minor pile-up of bodies. Finding Fred, he said, "How about I bring my dogs back here? They might lead us to Kate and Helen."

"Worth a try," Fred conceded. "Ring me, when you're on your way back."

# CHAPTER THIRTY-FIVE

Kate screwed her eyes tightly shut as she gradually gained consciousness. Her head throbbed, making her feel sick. Groaning, her first coherent thought was, let me die now. She had no intention of moving her aching head or opening her eyes to the possibility of bright sunlight. She had no idea why she felt as sick as she did and didn't even want to try to remember what she'd done to deserve such a bad hangover with no recollection of how she'd achieved it.

She reasoned that she must have slept awkwardly, as her right shoulder was in spasm. Concentrating on keeping her head still and her eyes closed, she tried to release her shoulder from underneath her. Confused and disorientated, she closed her eyes tighter. She couldn't move her shoulder. Something was blocking it. When she tried harder, a sharp stabbing pain ran up her wrist and along her arm. She tugged again at her shoulder, trying to turn over in the bed. What the hell?

She tried opening one eye. A kaleidoscope of bright, pinpricks of light dancing in a black void assaulted her senses, and she quickly closed it again. Bile rose in her throat. She feared she was going to vomit at any moment. She had to wriggle around onto her stomach.

She started to panic as it dawned on her that something was terribly wrong. She couldn't move either arm. They were pinned tightly behind her back, which explained the searing pain shooting through her shoulders and ending in her throbbing head. Terrified, she started to hyperventilate. Gasping for air, she realised something was blocking her mouth. She needed air, but nothing was coming through. Her lungs ached with the strain of trying to draw in air. The dancing lights speeded up, spinning and swirling in manic circles behind her closed eyes. She was ordering her body to thrash about and free itself, but nothing was moving. Had she been in an accident? Was she paralysed? Where were the doctors and nurses? Shouldn't they be rushing to her bedside? Wouldn't alarms on whatever machine she was hooked up to be going crazy by now?

Her brain told her she could breathe through her nose, but her mouth continued in its futile attempts to take in air. She had to get herself under control and stop panicking. Calmly work out how to escape from wherever she was trapped. Terror pushed down on her chest. Had she been buried alive? Forcing her eyes open didn't help. All around her was black. The air she breathed in was dusty. There was a musty smell she thought she recognised but couldn't quite identify. She wriggled side to side to see. Probing to see if she would come up against the hard sides of the coffin. Whatever contained her was soft and giving. She'd never seen an open coffin other than in films. They were lined, weren't they? Normally, the occupants wouldn't care how soft their final resting place was. She guessed the lining was for the benefit of mourners. Or maybe it was to stop the body from rolling around and making a distressing sound as it was carried to its final resting place. Only this wasn't a normal service. She was alive. She had to find a way to let people know. Forgetting about breathing through her nose, she tried to fill up her lungs, ready to start screaming for help. Her chest ached with the effort. The pain and terror disappeared as blackness took over once more as she slipped back into unconsciousness.

The ecstatically happy dogs leapt all over Simon, licking every available piece of bare flesh they could find. Their joy lifted Simon's dark mood for a brief moment. He completed the paperwork while the stern receptionist reprimanded him about allowing his dogs to roam freely without collars. She handed him a card for dog training classes, pointing out that farmers shot out-of-control dogs and how if they'd caused a road traffic accident, he would be liable as their owner. Not wanting to be held up any longer than needed, Simon smiled politely, nodded in all the right places and paid a ridiculously inflated price for two leads. Hurrying towards the exit, he made a point of throwing the card in the wastepaper bin, knowing the miserable woman was watching.

Once in the car, he telephoned Fred to say he was on his way back. Fred told him the police dogs were struggling to pick out Kate's scent. Although classed as a slow day, still hundreds of people had visited the park earlier. Many more had turned up to help with the search. All of which made picking out one person's scent more difficult.

As pre-arranged, Fred met him in the car park. Fred pointed to their left, explaining the dogs had been taken out onto the trails and were working clockwise in the hope they would pick something up away from the main entrance. Simon pulled back the sliding door to the rear of the camper van, and Alfred and Albert jumped out. Realising where they were, both dogs stared intently at a path leading away to their right.

Simon bent down to pat them. "Is that where Kate is? Go find Kate!"

Fred looked down at the two dogs, furiously wagging their tails while staring up at Simon. "Have they got any tracking experience?"

Simon shrugged. "Well, no. But I still think they might lead us straight to where they were parted from Kate and Helen." Turning back to the dogs, he swung his right arm in an arc. "Go find Kate! Go on!"

The dogs sprang forward towards a path on their far right. Every so often, they turned to check Simon and Fred were following, before running on again.

"They seem to have a clear destination in mind," Fred conceded. "And they seem keen for us to follow them. Let's hope they're not leading us to where they gave chase to a bunch of rabbits earlier today."

Knowing how partial they were to chasing rabbits and deer unless called back immediately, Simon pushed that knowledge to the back of his mind and marched on. "I'm sure they're on to something," he said, a short while later, small bubbles of excitement forming. They weren't darting off to explore new smells but were moving forward purposefully.

Panting, to keep up with Simon, Fred said, "I hope so. Did you have a chat with Richard?"

Simon shook his head, his eyes never leaving the two dogs. "I left before they arrived home. Sorry. I couldn't sit around doing nothing in that empty house." Nodding towards the dogs, he added, "Not when I could be more useful out here."

Fred pulled out a battered map of the park and his phone. Breathlessly he said into the phone, "The lad's dogs seem to be on to something. They've led us out on Barn Walk and are heading towards an area called Cherry Grove. Could I have a search party follow us out this way?" After a brief silence, he added, "Can I speak to anyone who searched out this way earlier on?" He completed the call and made another one to his son, "Hi Tom. We think we might have something out on Barn Walk. Can you tell me, what's out this way?"

The dogs came to a fork in the path. Without hesitating, they took the left pathway. "That's interesting," Fred said. "Tom said, if the dogs take the left path, we'll go deeper into the woods, and we'll come across a shed where they store their Christmas paraphilia off to our right. It's not used for anything else and is rarely checked the rest of the year. A ranger did look inside earlier but didn't see anything. Tom is heading this way on a quad bike with the key to the shed to recheck it. He confirmed the phone signal is intermittent out there, but with a bit of walking around, you can normally get one."

The light was fading fast when they entered the woods. Simon shivered, wishing he'd grabbed a jacket on his way out.

Fred glanced across at him. "Want me to ask Tom to bring a spare Rangers jacket out with him?"

"No, it'll only waste time, and it's starting to get dark."

"Don't worry about that, son. I've got a torch, and we can jump on the back of the quad bike once Tom catches us up." They marched on in silence for a while. "This girl, Kate. I'm guessing she means a lot to you?"

Simon quickened his pace, intently watching the ground for tree roots and uneven areas. "She's a friend. I care about all my friends."

Fred risked saying, "I got the impression, she was someone special. More than a friend," before they lapsed into silence.

Up ahead, the dogs had stopped and were sniffing around the edge of the track. Simon broke into a run. He could hear the ragged breathing of Fred as he pounded along behind him. The dogs glanced back at them as they approached and started to bark. In the distance, they heard the roar of a quad bike coming closer.

# CHAPTER THIRTY-SIX

Mark rubbed his aching neck. He'd lost track of time since hearing Simon leave, and his scrunched-up position in the corner of the cupboard was increasingly uncomfortable. He moved his hand to the dull pain in his right hip, rubbing it in a circular motion. The air was stale and dusty. A couple of times, he'd had to stifle a dry cough. He was considering moving the suitcases to adjust his position when he heard the front door opening and closing.

He strained to hear the muffled voices. Initially, he caught only the odd word, but as he concentrated harder, he could make out strings of words. He silently congratulated himself on his correct prediction before pushing himself hard against the back wall.

"We'll check all the rooms before we leave. The two officers will remain outside until the morning."

"What will happen in the morning?"

"They'll check you had a good night's sleep, after being relieved by two more officers."

"Thank you. Can I get you anything to eat or drink?"

"We're fine, thank you."

"How about the officers outside?"

"They'll be fine as well. They might appreciate a cup of tea and a bacon sandwich in the morning, but for now, leave them to do their job."

"Yes. Yes, of course. And someone will let us know if my daughter is found."

"I'm sure they will. Bill, here, will go and search upstairs while I'll check downstairs."

"The living room is through there. Should we wait here?"

"Once I've checked the living room is clear you can follow me through."

◆ ◆ ◆

Heavy footsteps pounding above him, blocked out the conversation. The thud, thud of the officer's boots reverberated in Mark's chest. He locked his arms tightly around his legs and pulled his knees towards him. So close they pressed into his chest, hampering his already laboured breathing. He wished they'd started their search in the hallway. The anticipation was killing him. His palms were so sweaty he stopped moving the knife from hand to hand in case it accidentally slipped from his hand and clattered to the floor, giving his location away. He worried the rasping sound of his breathing might do that, anyway.

The thud, thud stopped. The creaking floorboards and the clicks of doors opening and closing above him became fainter until they disappeared completely. He strained to hear anything over his ragged breathing. He tried to control his breath until he felt his heart would explode. He wondered which he would hear first, the thud of the officer descending the stairs or the other one re-entering the hallway. He leaned forward in the hope it would improve his hearing.

He gasped in agony as a cramp shot up through his left calf. He bit down hard and screwed his eyes shut to stop himself from shouting out in pain as he furiously rubbed his leg. He wanted to kick out at the suitcases and walk about to ease the cramp. Impatiently, he asked himself what they were doing out there. A vision of an overweight officer lounging on a kitchen chair with a hot cup of tea and a plate of homemade scones in front of him filled his mind. The painful cramp was making it harder to breathe as he became increasingly irritated by the thought of the officer leisurely taking time.

A few weeks before the end, Betty had cried out in the night with unbearable cramps in her legs and feet. He'd sat for hours at the end of the bed, trying to massage her pain away. If he could have sucked in all her pain along with the evil cancer, he would have done so willingly. He didn't believe in God, but he'd prayed every night for a miracle. Betty was the warmest, kindest person he'd ever met. She didn't deserve any of it. Mark's resolve hardened when he thought of the added pain his son, and the selfish monster outside had caused. Once he'd prayed to take on Betty's agony, yet here he was whimpering over a bit of cramp.

He briefly forgot to breathe when footsteps crossed the stone floor. He chastised himself. He had to get a grip and control his emotions. The door to the cupboard clicked open, and light danced around him above his head. He pressed his eyes shut and hugged his knees, willing the officer to move away. Thud, thud, thud announced the other officer coming down the stairs.

"All clear upstairs."

"Everything appears to be in order down here."

The light went out, and the door clicked shut. More footsteps. An internal door opening.

"We've completed our search. We'll see ourselves out. Try to get some sleep."

The front door opened and shuddered shut.

Mark breathed deeply in and out and relaxed his hold on his knees. Alone at last, proud of his ability to avoid detection, he thought about how far he'd come. The years he'd wasted being meek and mild, choosing to turn the other cheek while seething with anger inside at rude, inconsiderate people. The people who pushed in front of him in queues, noisy neighbours who slammed their doors in the early hours of the morning, parents who allowed their screaming children to destroy his peace and work colleagues who belittled him. The list was endless. He wouldn't stand for it anymore. If he escaped to a new life, things would be different. He would be different. No! Not if, when.

He pushed the large suitcase away and stretched out his legs. The cramp had gone, but the crick in his neck remained. He shifted along to the centre of the cupboard where space wasn't so restricted and waited, counting over and over again, to one hundred until he'd lost count. It was apparent Richard, and Alicia were not going to head upstairs to bed anytime soon. He replaced his plan to murder them in their sleep with something far bolder.

He slipped the knife into his pocket and slowly got to his feet. He hesitated and pushed against the door. The click of the door opening sounded like a firecracker going off. He froze in the doorway, listening for sounds of movement. Hearing nothing, he slipped through the door. Leaving it ajar to avoid another click, he quickly made his way across the stone floor. His rubber-soled walking boots made a quiet thwack with each step.

He pressed his ear to the door, but he still couldn't hear anything on the other side. He had to make his move at some point. He felt in his pocket for the syringes. Satisfied they were in place, he grasped the door handle, slowly turning it. He took a deep breath and eased the door open, just far enough to peer inside the next room. It was a large open-planned living room with a dining area to the right, lit only by one small table lamp. He sensed movement in the dining area and broke out in a sweat. He let out a sigh of relief when he realised it was the internal workings of the water mill behind a glass case.

An interior door at the far end of the room had been left ajar, and a narrow ribbon of light marked the corner of the room. Mark cautiously crept forward, carefully placing each foot in front of the other as though walking along a tightrope suspended high in the air. He pressed himself against the wall once he'd managed to cross the room.

He furtively looked through the open door into a kitchen filled with chrome gadgetry. The kitchen was empty. Patio doors at the far end were fully open, the curtains rising and falling in the breeze. Richard and Alicia were sitting at an outside table on the patio, enjoying a bottle of red wine.

Mark withdrew from the doorway. He stood with his back pressed against the wall. 'What sort of people were they? Their daughter is missing, and they're laughing and joking while sharing an expensive red wine. They deserve to die for their callousness.'

# CHAPTER THIRTY-SEVEN

The dogs glanced once more at Simon before disappearing to their right. Simon screeched to a halt, watching where they went. He half-slid, half-ran down the steep bank towards a long, low wooden outbuilding. He came to a stop in front of a padlocked door where the dogs were frantically scratching. Fred came careering down the bank, stopping only when he collided headfirst with the side of the building. Behind him, his son carefully manoeuvred the quad bike down the steep bank.

Fred shouted, "Wasn't this shed checked earlier?"

Tom jumped off the quad bike and jogged to join them. "Yes. Nothing seemed out of place, but they did remove the key that is normally hanging there," he said, pointing to a spot beneath the roof's overhang. Holding up a small silver key, Tom added, "I've got it here." He inserted it into the padlock, which popped open on well-oiled springs. He pulled back the catch and opened the door.

Simon pushed past Tom and was the first to enter. He came face to face with a gigantic sleigh that took up most of the available space. He started to edge around it when the dogs galloped into the room. They ran over the top of the sleigh and dived into a pile of hollow boxes decorated to look like oversized Christmas presents. Simon dived after them and started rummaging through the boxes, throwing them back out over his shoulder. Beneath the boxes were two large hessian sacks. One of which appeared to be moving. "Over here!"

Simon felt the contours of the moving sack and knew there

was a person inside. He grabbed the rope tying it shut, but he could neither undo nor remove it. Something inside the sack shifted again. He was about to cry out in frustration when Fred appeared at his side with a sharp penknife. "Here, take this. Tom has another one."

Simon cut the rope cleanly and pulled open the sack. He looked directly into Kate's terrified eyes. Without thinking, he grabbed the end of the duct tape across her mouth and ripped it away. He held her upright by her shoulders while she gasped for air. The sack fell away to reveal her arms were tied behind her back. As soon as he cut the rope binding her wrists, she threw her arms around his neck and held on tightly. Every part of her was shaking as her arms remained locked around his neck, her tears wetting his face. Simon closed his eyes and hugged her back. They'd been here before, shortly after they made the crossing to France. Then, like now, she'd let down her guard and had needed him. The difference then was she was drunk, and he hadn't realised how much he needed her. She was the reason he carried on living.

Without warning, Kate released him and moved back. "Helen!"

Helen had been released from her sack and laid out on the floor in the recovery position. They heaved a joint sigh of relief when they saw twitches of movement. Helen abruptly raised her head and was sick all over Tom's shoes. Tom jumped back and stamped his feet as though that would remove the vomit. Helen put both hands to her head and groaned, "My head. I think it's going to explode."

The search team that Fred had called earlier piled through the doorway as he pulled out his phone to call for an ambulance. He shouted at them. "Stay outside. This is a crime scene. Make sure no one else, except the paramedics, tries to come in." Next, he called the station asking for officers to secure the area. He turned to Kate, "Can you tell us what happened?"

Kate dried her eyes and face on her sleeve. "Not really." Her body was racked by a huge sob. "I thought I'd been buried alive. I couldn't see or breathe."

Simon pulled her protectively towards him. "Do we have to do this now?"

Fred looked sympathetic, but said, "Anything you could tell us would help. We still don't know for sure, who is responsible."

Simon started to say something, but Kate spoke over him. "Sorry. I don't remember anything at all. One moment we were walking along, chatting happily. Next." She spread her arms out wide. "We're here."

"It was Mark Oates, I tell you," Simon said.

"Mark? The man who called the ambulance for Richard? No!" Kate said.

"Yes, him," Simon said, bitterly. "I'll tell you about it later. I only found out after you left. I didn't think for one minute he'd be following you."

With wide unbelieving eyes, Kate asked, "And Richard and Alicia?"

"They're at home with police officers guarding the front and rear of the house."

"But why?"

Approaching sirens wailed outside in the distance.

"That'll be either the ambulance or more police," Fred said.

"For Helen?" Kate asked.

"For you as well. You need to be checked over," Fred replied. "They'll need to do blood tests, if nothing else, to establish what you were both given."

Kate's eyes pleaded with Simon. "I feel fine. I'll only be in the way at the hospital. They'll probably discharge me straight away, anyway." She looked back at Fred. Squeezing Simon's hand, she said, "I want to go home. This isn't about me. It's about Richard, Alicia and Helen. I was just unlucky enough to get caught up in the crossfire. Collateral damage, or whatever you call it."

Looking between Kate and Fred, Simon said, "How about we ask the ambulance crew to check you over, here? Leave it to them to say whether you're fit to go home?" Pushing the remaining boxes out of the way, he took a firm hold of her elbow and added, "Let's see if you can walk out of here, first."

After cutting the rope from her ankles, Simon guided Kate out past the heap of boxes. Helen vomited again, just before they heard the ambulances arrive. When Simon led Kate through the door, they were blinded by the flashing blue lights. Four paramedics in green jumpsuits were sliding their way down the steep slope. Two disappeared inside the shed while the remaining two helped Simon and Kate climb back up the slope. At Simon's request, they sat Kate in the rear of the ambulance while they measured her vital signs and probed her eyes with a bright penlight. Kate continued to insist she was feeling fine and wanted to go home. Finally, they gave their verdict. "We can't force you, but we'd be happier if you went into hospital to be fully assessed."

Kate smiled and slid from the edge of the bed. "In other words, you think I'm okay. You want to cover yourselves in case I sue. I promise I won't. Can I go now?"

Sighing, the elder of the two paramedics replied, "You're acting against our best advice." Stepping back, he added, "If you are happy to sign a disclaimer to that effect, then we can't stop you from leaving."

Kate's smile grew. "Where's the form?"

Simon started to object, but one look from Kate told him it was pointless. He said to the paramedic, "I'll take good care of her. Is there anything I should be looking out for?"

"Without knowing what she's been given, it's hard to say."

"Hello! She's here," Kate interrupted.

Ignoring her, the paramedic said, "Anything that causes you to worry. Nausea, sudden drowsiness, vomiting, severe headache, difficulty breathing, raised heart rate." Looking severely at Kate, he added, "Anything really."

Their attention was drawn to one of the other paramedics, followed by Fred hurrying up the bank.

"Is Helen, okay?" Kate asked.

Without stopping, the paramedic continued to the rear of the ambulance. "Violently sick and a severe headache," Fred said between pants, helping to pull the folded stretcher from the ambulance.

Passing them again before returning down the bank, the paramedic said, "We'll get her to the hospital to be fully assessed as quickly as possible."

"As you should be," Kate's paramedic said, handing her a form on a clipboard with a pen attached by a piece of string.

Kate quickly signed and returned it. Turning to Simon, she said, "Please, take me home."

Fred rejoined them. "You're returning to Clenchers Mill, then?" When they both nodded, he said, "I'll let the officers stationed out there know. Otherwise, they won't let you through."

Simon thanked him and held out his hand to Kate, "Come on, but don't you dare have a funny turn on me."

Kate pulled a face, but took his hand and replied, "Deal." Checking her pockets, she stopped and looked down the bank to the shed. "Damn! I must have dropped my phone. I wanted to call Alicia to tell her about Helen."

Simon pulled out his phone and waved it around above his head. "Wouldn't do you any good. There's no signal out here." Pocketing the phone, he added, "If Mark hasn't taken it, the police will find and return your phone." Walking on, he said, "I'll try again later." Giving Kate a sly grin, he said, "Alicia will probably want me to take her to visit Helen. As I can't have you out of my sight, you'll have to come with us. You may as well get checked out there, while we're waiting to see Helen."

"Can't they drive themselves?" Kate asked.

"In what? As far as I'm aware, Richard's Porsche is wrapped around a tree somewhere, Alicia's mini has two, slashed rear tyres, and she's done nothing about replacing the smashed windscreen on the Range Rover."

Tom on his quad bike, roared towards them. Stopping next to them, he said, "Jump on the back. I'll take you back to your camper van."

# CHAPTER THIRTY-EIGHT

Frustration was getting the better of Mark. Not only had Richard and Alicia remained at the patio table, but every so often they waved to someone. Mark guessed it was the officer guarding the rear of the house. He rechecked the time when a shrill ring and a quiet, knocking sound pulled him up sharp. In the semi-light, a mobile phone vibrated on a low table by one of the plump sofas.

At last. He was as ready as he was ever going to be. He pressed his back into the wall behind the door and pulled a syringe from his pocket.

He felt remarkably calm when he heard approaching footsteps. Too light to be Richard's. He guessed it was Alicia rushing to answer her phone, hoping for good news about her daughter. He took a deep breath to centre himself. A heavy perfume proceeded her through the doorway, confirming yet another correct guess. Once she was fully through the door, Mark grabbed her from behind. His left hand closed over her mouth while his right plunged the syringe into the top of her arm. He felt her warm body sway before her legs gave out. He managed to pull her a few steps to the side before she completely lost consciousness, and he lowered her to the floor. He shot across the room to silence the phone. For good measure, he switched it off before returning to his position behind the door.

Knowing Richard would soon follow Alicia through the doorway when she didn't return, he quickly dragged her lifeless body to the side, out of a direct line of sight from the doorway. He returned to his post to wait.

Slow minutes ticked by. Alicia looked like the type of person who chatted for hours on the phone with her friends. The heartless way they'd relaxed outside sharing a bottle of wine confirmed they weren't worried about her daughter or the other woman. The way she'd strolled across to answer the phone suggested a complete lack of urgency. A caring mother would have had her mobile to hand, desperate for news. Sighing, he accepted he could be in for another long wait.

Mark rolled his eyes when, after another five minutes had passed, he heard Richard shouting for his wife. Mark muttered under his breath, "Come on, you lazy bastard. Get off your fat behind and come and see why your wife hasn't returned." The home phone on a windowsill next to an armchair rang. Heavier footsteps and the tapping noise of a crutch crossed the kitchen floor. Mark smiled as he readied himself behind the door.

◆ ◆ ◆

Travelling through the narrow lanes, Kate stared at Simon's phone screen in confusion. "That's odd. I keep getting the same message, that the number is temporarily unavailable. Please, try again later."

Simon pressed down harder on the accelerator. "We'll be there in a couple of minutes." Forcing his voice to remain calm, he added, "Alicia might have decided to get a new phone after all the unpleasant text messages she received. I'm pretty sure I added the home number. Give that a go."

Scrolling alphabetically through Simon's contacts, Kate said, "Nothing else coming up for Alicia or Clenchers Mill."

"I probably entered it under Richard's name."

"Got it!" With the phone pressed to her ear, Kate said, "It's ringing."

Simon slowed on the approach to the closed gate. A uniformed police constable raised his hand in greeting and opened the gate for them. He lowered the window to thank him before accelerating along the driveway. He glanced across at Kate, still holding the phone to her ear.

Kate shook her head and disconnected the call. "They're not answering. Why didn't you tell the guy at the gate to come in with us?"

Bringing the car to a standstill, Simon said, "You haven't spent the last few hours with Fred Collins. He may look slow, but he thinks of everything. I wouldn't be at all surprised to discover he called them and arranged a car to take them to the hospital, half an hour ago."

Slamming her car door as she climbed out, Kate said, across the roof of the car, "Then, why didn't you ask the guy at the gate whether they left?"

Simon scratched the back of his head. "I didn't think of that." He pulled out his key and inserted it into the lock. Flicking on the hallway lights, he shouted, "Alicia! Richard! Anyone home?"

Fred Collins pulled out his phone as he watched the rear of the ambulance disappear. He walked a few steps along the track before he picked up a signal. He rang PC Robert Fall to check all was quiet at Clenchers Mill and to tell him two vehicles would be arriving shortly. A squad car to take Richard and Alicia to the hospital and a camper van. Ending that call, he called Alicia to give her the good news. The phone rang and rang while he walked in small circles, before cutting out. He immediately redialled the number. This time, receiving the message that the phone was temporarily unavailable.

He rang the station, advising Kate and Helen had been found, but he needed someone to head for Clenchers Mill immediately as the mother wasn't answering the phone. Next, he rang his son, shouting at him to get back and pick him up on the quad bike. It occurred to him that Simon may have telephoned ahead to tell Alicia that her daughter was on the way to the hospital. That would explain why their phone wasn't being answered. He relaxed until he realised that if they'd left, PC Fall would have mentioned it.

He considered sending the two PCs guarding the property in to check everything was in order. He decided against it. He didn't want them blundering about in there until they knew what they were dealing with. If there was a problem, it would be better for them to follow in the more experienced officers he'd already requested.

# CHAPTER THIRTY-NINE

As they entered the silent hallway, Simon hoped he was right about Fred calling ahead, but small seeds of doubt lodged in the back of his brain. "Why don't you wait in the car? I'll double-check they're not here, and we can head out to the hospital to find them."

"I'm here now. I may as well check they're not here, with you," Kate replied.

"You could go back and speak to the guy on the gate?" Simon suggested. Before he could react, Kate dashed past him and swung open the door to the living room. It took a while for Simon's confused, tired brain to make sense of what he saw over Kate's shoulder. In a daze, he stepped into the room and tried to push Kate back behind him, toward the doorway.

"Neither of you moves, or I'll slit her throat." Mark was crouched on the floor between Richard and Alicia, both laid out flat on the floor on their backs. Mark held the edge of a serrated hunting knife to Alicia's throat.

Still trying to drag Kate behind him, Simon said, "Okay. Okay. We're not going anywhere."

"Get the girl out where I can see her," Mark demanded.

Kate slowly stepped out to stand beside Simon, looking bewildered, "Why? You don't know them. You tried to help when Richard fell from his horse. You called the ambulance."

Simon stood rooted to the spot, wishing Kate would be quiet so he could think. This was bad. Really bad, but Mark couldn't kill all of them. He didn't care about himself, and this was all his fault anyway. Could Mark draw his knife across both of their throats in the time it would take him to cross the room? He could shout to Kate to run and get help so she would be safe. But could he cold-heartedly sacrifice two people for her?

Mark spoke directly to Kate. "He stole my son. Not just from me, but from Betty. He couldn't even be bothered to visit her before she died. Every day she asked when he was coming. No matter what I did to ease her pain, it was him she cried for."

"I don't understand," Kate said, looking increasingly confused. "Betty? Is that your wife? She's dead? I thought you moved here together. How could he have stolen your son? Presumably, he had a mind of his own?"

Simon dug Kate in the ribs, before reaching for her hand and squeezing it tight. This wasn't helping. The mix of pain, anger and frustration on Mark's face was chilling. Kate was pushing him further and further over the edge.

Kate hesitated, before asking, "How did Richard steal your son?"

When Mark replied, it was as though only he and Kate were in the room. "He introduced him to a different lifestyle of ease and glamour. One we couldn't afford. All we ever heard was Richard this and Richard that. After all the sacrifices we made for him. Betty nearly died carrying him. I said, never again. The risk was too great."

"That wasn't stealing him, though, was it?" Kate said.

"To keep him, he got him hooked on drugs. David's brain was so addled he couldn't think past where his next fix was coming from."

"But I saw the photographs in your house. You all looked so happy."

"That was before,"

"So, where is your son, really?" Kate asked.

Simon took a sharp intake of breath. He had to do something to stop this, while Mark's attention was focused solely on Kate.

Mark's face clouded over. Angrily, he spat out, "Dead, as I told you."

Kate took a step forward. "I'm sorry for your loss, but ..."

Mark pointed the knife at her. "Get back! I killed him, and I'm going to kill the lot of you."

Simon pulled Kate back. Out of the corner of his eye, he saw movement through the open door. Fred was making his way through the fluttering curtains from the patio to the kitchen. His eyes snapped back to Mark. He prayed he'd been quick enough, and he hadn't given Fred away. He glanced across at Kate. He felt her trembling. Now that she understood the situation they'd walked in on, she froze. It was up to him to continue what she'd started. He had to draw Mark's attention. Keep him talking for just a few minutes more.

Mark shifted position and pressed the knife against Richard's throat, instead of Alicia's. The pressure on his neck increased, and a dribble of blood trickled to the floor. "Don't waste your sympathy on my son. I put him out of his misery when he finally decided to put in an appearance. When it was too late. Feeling sorry for himself. Expecting me to feel pity for him."

Simon could see that while Mark's eyes remained locked on Kate, the pressure on Richard's throat was increasing. "Alicia hasn't done anything to harm you. And what about Helen, her daughter? You'll be depriving her of her mother," he said.

Mark threw his head back to laugh, the knife digging deeper into Richard's throat, increasing the blood flow. "That little harlot! Happy to pose naked for the first boy who showed any interest in her. Like mother, like daughter. Neither will be a loss to the gene pool."

Simon fixed his eyes on Mark, willing him to stop, but knowing he wouldn't. Wanting to look away but feeling compelled to watch. He felt Kate tense. He could sense the cogs of her brain turning over this new information. Realising Mark was the mastermind behind the sex-texting.

"You!" Mark shouted. His deranged eyes fixed on Simon. "I can see what you're thinking. Will he have time to slit both their throats in the time it would take me to reach him?" Lifting the knife slightly, preparing to make the final cut, a crazy smile, lit his face. "Let's see, shall we?"

A blur of green flashed across the scene as Fred flung himself at Mark. Simon was unable to see whether the desperate rugby tackle had been in time. Fred and Mark rolled across the floor. The knife propelled across the floor was dripping blood. Time stood still, as Simon remained rooted to the spot, fixated by the bloodstains.

"Get the bloody knife! Goddammit!" Fred shouted.

Shocked into action, Simon shot across the room to retrieve the knife. Kate pulled off her T-shirt. Kneeling in her bra, she scrunched it into a ball and held it against Richard's throat. Suddenly, the room was full of people, shouting orders and taking over. Fred was dragged off Mark, who was quickly handcuffed and led from the room. Someone was shouting into a phone. "Ambulance. Quick." Another pulled the knife from Simon's frozen hand and slid it into a see-through plastic bag. Kate was being pulled up and away from Richard. She looked bewildered and lost in her underwear, red stains on her trainers and the knees of her jeans. Her white T-shirt, rapidly turning red, was being pressed against Richard's neck by other hands.

Simon took off his sweatshirt and draped it around Kate's shoulders, whispering to her, as much for his benefit as hers, "It's okay. It's all over now."

Holding on to one another, they were gently pushed from the room into the kitchen. More people flooded in, including an ambulance crew. The door to the living room closed as they sat in silence. Time stood still as shock kicked in. They clung to each other as they both shook uncontrollably.

# CHAPTER FORTY

After the celebratory meal, it was midday by the time the camper van was loaded up and the keys to the cottage handed back. Their second week had been far more relaxing and uneventful than the first. Richard, Alicia and Helen piled out of Clenchers Mill to say goodbye.

Richard shook Simon's and Kate's hands. "Like I said in the hospital, I'll help you in any way I can. If I hear of anyone needing the services of private investigators, I'll be sure to recommend you two," he said, in a croaky voice.

"Four! What about the role Alfred and Albert played?" Helen pointed out, scratching the two dogs.

"I stand corrected. Four," Richard agreed.

Looking across at Simon, Kate said, "Three. I've had enough excitement to last a lifetime. I think I'm going to concentrate on becoming a professional groom and house-sitter. That sounds far less dangerous."

"We might take you up on that," Richard said. "Once we're fully recovered, I think we deserve a holiday. Where do you fancy?"

"New York," Helen said.

"Iceland," Alicia said.

"Oh. I was thinking of a beach holiday," Richard said, faking disappointment at their choices.

Simon slid back the rear door of the camper van, and the two dogs jumped in, wagging their tails. "Good luck with deciding where you're going." Closing the rear door and jumping into the driver's seat, Simon said, "We'd be happy to house-sit if I haven't a case on the go."

"Thank you, again," Alicia said, as Simon lowered the window and Kate climbed in from the other side. "See you both again very soon."

The three stood back, waving as Simon started the engine. Helen mouthed, "Thank you," and Simon winked back in reply, before driving away.

Once clear of the gates, Simon said, "House-sitting? How boring. Dealing with the drudgery other people are escaping from, while they're away having fun. Probably being nipped by darling little Fifi, who's far too precious to go into kennels like a regular dog."

"I thought we could specialise in taking on more than dogs. Families with horses, chickens and goats. That sort of thing. Maybe, even small holdings or other small businesses."

"Really?" Simon replied, with a pained expression.

"Yes, really."

As Kate settled back in her seat, a broad grin spread across Simon's face. He didn't care what they did, as long as he had a part in Kate's life.

# OTHER BOOKS BY DIANA J FEBRY

Trouble at Fatting House
Trouble at Suncliffe Manor
Trouble at Sharcott

Detective Series

The Skeletons of Birkbury
Bells on her Toes
Point of no Return
Who Killed Vivien Morse?
Twisted Truth
The Paperboy

A Fiery End
A Mother's Ruin
A Relative Death
An Educated Death
A Deadly Drop
A Sudden Death